Secret Behind Locked Doors

Connie Griffith and her family live in Boone, North Carolina. She and her husband serve at the headquarters of Africa Evangelical Fellowship. This is her first series of American children's novels.

The Tootie McCarthy Series

BOOK 3

Secret Behind
Locked Doors

Connie Griffith

A Division of Baker Book House Co
Grand Rapids, Michigan 49516

Cover illustration by Jim Hsieh, © 1994 Baker Book House

Published by Baker Books
a division of Baker Book House Company
P.O. Box 6287, Grand Rapids, Michigan 49516-6287

Printed in the United States of America

Library of Congress Cataloging-in-Publication Data

Griffith, Connie
    Secret behind locked doors / Connie Griffith.
       p. cm. — (The Tootie McCarthy series : bk. 3)
    Sequel to: Surprise at Logan School.
    Sequel: Mysterious rescuer.
    Summary: Early in 1928, thirteen-year-old Tootie McCarthy's mother
becomes very ill, so her parents decide to send Tootie's younger brother,
a Mongoloid, to an asylum run by a doctor Tootie does not trust.
    ISBN 0-8010-3864-2
    [1. Irish American—Fiction. 2. Mentally handicapped—Fiction. 3.
Family life—Fiction. 4. Christian life—Fiction.] I. Title. II. Series: Griffith, Connie. Tootie McCarthy series ; bk. 3.
    G88175Se 1994
    [Fic]—dc20   93-8420

Scripture quotations are from the King James Version of the Bible.

To my uncle
Ralph "Buddy" Spellman
and all other learning disabled individuals
who have been mistreated

Tootie bit down on her lower lip to keep from giggling in her ninth-grade mathematics lesson. But it was awfully hard not to laugh at the way Miss Penick was throwing her long, thin arms round and round in the air as she tried explaining a particularly difficult word problem.

"Watch out! S-she's going to take f-flight," Joey Staddler whispered. He sat in the seat directly behind Tootie, who sat in the front row beneath the flailing arms of Miss Penick.

Tootie pressed her hand over her mouth, trying desperately not to burst into laughter at Joey's comment. Then she turned slightly in the old bolted-down seat and glanced over her shoulder at her best friend. Her legs were too short for the ninth-grade desks, and her feet dangled about an inch from the hardwood floor.

Just then Miss Penick's bony hand landed forcefully, palm down, on Tootie's desk. She bent her tall frame forward and demanded, "Will you share this little joke with the class, Miss McCarthy?"

Tootie could feel her face flush. She heard several girls snicker. "I'm sorry, ma'am," Tootie said, staring nervously at her mathematics book. All of a sudden, the way her teacher flung her arms through the air didn't seem quite as funny.

"We are waiting," Miss Penick said and stood erect with her arms folded across her chest. "What did you say to Joey Staddler?"

"Nothing, ma'am," Tootie responded in a respectful tone. "Honestly, I didn't say anything." That was the truth. Joey had been the one who'd talked.

"Hmmmm. . . ." Miss Penick sounded hesitant. "Well, whatever's going on, I have no doubt that you're at the bottom of it, Miss McCarthy."

Several girls snickered again. Tootie knew without looking that one of them was Irene. Even before Tootie had sneaked the Gypsies into the school play, Irene had been against her.

"Quit waving your hand at me," Miss Penick said to Joey. "I don't want to hear any explanations from you. All you try to do these days is defend this one." The grouchy teacher jabbed her thumb toward Tootie.

Then Miss Penick turned and walked back to her desk. "Class," she announced as she straightened the already-straight pile of papers on her fancy desk pad, "because this interchange has taken up valuable learning time, your homework will be increased." Miss Penick began writing the assignment on the blackboard.

"That's not fair!" Irene grumbled loudly. Others agreed.

Just then the dismissal bell rang.

Tootie couldn't believe it. *Why is Miss Penick always picking on me? What have I done? I can't stand much more with everything else that's going on—*

Joey nudged her slender shoulder. "S-sorry, Tootie."

She shrugged and picked up her books, determined not to let Irene and the others know how upset she felt. "Wish we didn't have to hurry home," Tootie said, ignoring the glares of fellow classmates. "I'd love to go play some catch."

"Me, too!" Joey replied as he put on his black-and-white plaid jacket. Then he took Tootie's coat off the nail in the coat closet and handed it to her. "It's been ages s-since either one of us has done anything like that. I b-bet your little brother misses it, too."

Tootie felt choked with emotion. Her eight-year-old brother, Buddy, wasn't very smart, certainly not bright enough to go to school. He stayed home all the time. And with the difficulty their family had been having the past few months, Tootie knew her little brother's days were long and miserable. A game of catch would mean the world to him!

But instead of complaining, Tootie tied her red scarf under her chin then she and Joey hurried out of the classroom, down the hallway, and out the front entrance of Logan School. As they headed down the steps, Tootie said, "There will be no catch today, Joey. We both have work to do."

Joey nodded. Then he grinned proudly. "Did you

know I f-fixed that old bike? I'm delivering groceries for my d-dad."

"I've watched you zoom past the pie shop a few times with groceries piled so high on that bike of yours that you could hardly see," Tootie teased. "You're a crazy driver!"

Joey was about to defend himself when Pearl hurried over to them. "Hey, little sis," Pearl said, completely ignoring Joey. "I heard you got in trouble again in Miss Penick's class." Pearl was fifteen, two years older than Tootie. "Why do you always have to cause problems?"

Tootie could feel her Irish temper rising. She was determined not to get into an argument with Pearl, especially right there on Washington Street with Joey Staddler listening and everyone else hurrying by on their way home. Tootie just looked at her older sister without commenting. Pearl was pretty, all except for her front teeth. They were plastic. Sometimes when Pearl talked, her false front teeth moved downwards and a gap appeared between the plate and her gums.

Tootie looked away. She knew if Pearl caught her staring at her teeth, she'd be even more upset. Pearl was extremely sensitive about the one thing that marred her good looks, and it was her dream to get them properly fixed.

"I'll race you," Tootie suggested to Joey, knowing it would irritate her older sister. Pearl often complained that Tootie should grow up and act her age instead of playing catch or racing madly down city streets.

Joey grasped his books tightly and started to run.

Tootie followed. They darted together down the board-walk that ran the full length of Washington Street, one of the busiest streets in St. Paul, Minnesota. Tootie thought she saw Principal Harris pass in a new 1928 Model T automobile, but she didn't stop to check. She and Joey ran the four blocks with Tootie arriving first.

"You're still f-faster," Joey said, trying to catch his breath.

"See you tomorrow," Tootie giggled. Then she took off her scarf and shoved it into the pocket of her brown coat. "Be careful delivering groceries," she hollered as she pushed open the door to the McCarthy's Specialty Pie Bakery. The wind blew past her, swirling her short brown curls into tangles.

"Confound it, child!" a woman customer complained. "Shut that door!"

Tootie's books almost tumbled to the bakery floor as she kicked the door closed. "Hi, everyone," she greeted, and immediately recognized the complaining woman was Mrs. Peterson, Irene's mother.

Father stood behind the counter, dressed up as usual. He nodded and winked at Tootie, and then looked back at Mrs. Peterson who was bundled in a giant fur coat. "Excuse me, ma'am, what kind of pie did you order?"

"Apple!" she snapped. "I must say, Donald McCarthy, that if that bell above your door would quit ringing for one minute and if your little son weren't causing so much commotion over there in the corner, maybe you could hear me."

Tootie felt like hitting the terrible woman. How dare she talk like that!

Donald meticulously straightened his tie and smoothed the lapels of his dark suit. Tootie knew that her father always fidgeted when he was trying to control his temper.

Tootie hurried around the counter to see if she could stop her brother from making so much noise. Buddy was sitting on the floor banging his shoes against the wall saying over and over again, "Catch . . . catch . . . catch!"

For almost two months, Mother had been sick in bed in the family apartment above the bakery. She was not well enough to tend to Buddy, nor to help in the family business, so Father had to keep their young son down in the bakery all day. As a result, Buddy was constantly bored. Tootie felt like yelling all of this to the customers, especially to Irene's mother in her fancy furs. But Tootie knew Father wouldn't approve. He always said, "We McCarthys are proud people. We don't share our woes with just anybody!"

Tootie wanted to get Buddy away from the gawking customers and their rude comments. But she knew if she tried to quiet Buddy, or attempted to make him move fast, he'd get loud and stubborn. "Come on, Buddy Boy," Tootie urged, "let's go into the kitchen and see if Mrs. Roseen has any leftover apple peelings."

Suddenly Buddy clapped his hands and clumsily jumped to his feet. In doing so, he knocked a freshly baked apple pie right off the counter. It splattered all over the floor, and some of it got on Mrs. Peterson's fur coat.

"Why, you imbecile!" the woman shouted at Buddy. "I'm leaving! I'm sure there are plenty of other bakeshops in town."

"There are," Donald McCarthy responded, his temper no longer in check. "St. Paul, Minnesota, is full of them. I suggest you leave immediately!"

"Outrageous!" the woman sputtered.

For the next two hours Tootie tried to keep Buddy occupied in the bakery kitchen, help Mrs. Roseen finish her work, and then tidy the whole area. When the pie shop finally closed for the evening, she took Buddy upstairs to the family apartment and quickly made a bed for her mother on the sofa so she could be near the family during supper. "Is that comfortable, Mama?" Tootie asked after rearranging the pillows. "Is your stomach still upset?"

"Don't fuss, lass," Mother commented. "I'm feeling fine."

Tootie knew Mother wasn't fine. Her skin felt clammy and her eyes looked more deep-set than ever. Tootie smoothed a few graying hairs away from Mother's forehead. "Do you really think this is just the flu?"

Mother nodded her head, "Yes, I think it's the flu. And I'm definitely getting better." Eve tried to put on a brave smile.

Tootie glanced over at her sister, Pearl, who was placing the soup tureen by Father's end of the table. Their eyes met and they both knew the truth; Mother wasn't getting any better. Whatever was ailing her was not magically going away as they all wished. Even their prayers weren't helping. At least, that's how it seemed.

As soon as Pearl put the plate of sliced bread on the table, the meal was ready. Pearl sat across from Tootie and Buddy while Father presided at the head. He looked over toward the sofa and said as usual, "Evelyn, would you please give thanks for this delicious meal?"

Mother prayed so quietly that all Tootie could hear was the whispered, "Amen."

Immediately, Father began ladling the potato soup. It appeared thin and watery, and once again Tootie wished she could do the cooking while her older sister helped in the bakery. But she hid her feelings and carefully took the bowl from Father, placing it in front of Buddy. Then she buttered two slices of bread and put them on Buddy's plate.

Father offered her the next bowl with a mischievous grin. "Eat up, Tootie. This appears to be another of your sister's splendid successes."

Tootie knew Father was teasing, but it was obvious Pearl took him seriously. "Isn't it wonderful, Daddy?" she said. "I'm cooking like a grown woman. I bet you wouldn't even guess this is the first time I've ever made potato soup."

Donald took a small spoonful of the soup. Then he quickly picked up his napkin and dabbed at the corner of his mouth. "You've done it again, lass!"

Pearl's normally white skin flushed pink with pleasure. She wore her black hair parted down the middle, with each side coiled into a neatly pinned bun above the ear. It made her look so grown-up.

Buddy began dunking his bread in his bowl and slurping huge mouthfuls. "Mmmmmm," he moaned and took another messy mouthful. "Mmmmmm," he repeated, closing his eyes with obvious enjoyment.

The rest of the mealtime was filled with Father's talking. He believed that children were to be seen and not heard at the supper table. With Mother feeling ill, that meant Father had to carry on the entire conversation all by himself. But never once did he refer to the incident downstairs in the bakery when Buddy had knocked over the apple pie. In fact, Father was sounding quite optimistic. "This is 1928, and most businesses are booming. Our bakery business is bound to improve. By the way, I read that President Calvin Coolidge is going to run for another term of office in the upcoming election. That'll be good; he should be able to help this economy."

Just then Buddy emptied his bowl and, instead of asking for help, reached over to pick up the soup tureen. The large old-fashioned china bowl, one of the few fine pieces of china left from the days before they became so poor, slipped out of Buddy's stubby little fingers and hit the table with a crash. It broke wide open. Watery potato soup spread everywhere.

Pearl screamed.

Buddy began to cry.

Mother tried to get up from the sofa to come and help.

Father meticulously straightened the lapels of his dark

suit, and hurried into the bedroom. He quietly, but decisively, shut the door behind him.

Tootie took her cloth napkin and began cleaning up the mess. *Somehow things have got to get better,* Tootie thought and sighed deeply.

L ater that night, Tootie lay in bed next to Pearl. She pulled the wool blanket to her chin and wiggled further down into the saggy mattress. The moon shone through the thin curtains and caused weird shadows to dance on the wall across the room above Buddy's bed.

Buddy's snoring was often so loud that it kept Tootie awake. She stared at her brother's head on his pillow, wishing with all her heart that somehow he could be like other boys his age. She wanted to slip out from under the covers, run over to his bed, and give him a big hug.

After several minutes she whispered to Pearl, who was still restlessly trying to get comfortable, "Didn't you feel sorry for Buddy tonight when he broke our big china bowl?"

Pearl hit the mattress with her fist. "I was so mad I could have screamed! Why can't he be more careful? I loved that fancy tureen. That blue and purple flower design was so beautiful."

"I know," Tootie said, remembering how she had often traced her finger along the painted pansies. Just

17

having the tureen in the middle of the table somehow made potato soup taste better.

Pearl leaned up on her elbow, "Buddy's so clumsy. He makes me furious!"

"Pearl! It was an accident!" Tootie half-whispered, motioning for Pearl to keep her voice low.

"Oh, you always stick up for him," Pearl said.

"Shush! What if he wakes up and hears you?" Tootie glanced over toward Buddy's bed. He was still sound asleep. She didn't feel like talking with her sister tonight, so she pulled the covers up and sighed, pretending that she was settling down to sleep.

Pearl got the hint and turned over.

But Tootie didn't want to sleep. For the past few weeks, she'd heard her parents whispering late into the night. Their voices had a ring of urgency in them, and Tootie had a dreadful feeling something awful was about to happen.

After a while, Mother quietly came into the bedroom. Tootie closed her eyes and moved her head so that her face was almost hidden in the fluff of her pillow. She knew Mother could always tell when someone was faking. Eve walked over to check on Buddy, and then she crossed the room and stood over Tootie. It seemed as though she stood there forever. Pearl was on the other side of the bed, facing the wall. Her breathing had already become slow and even.

Finally Mother turned and slowly walked out of the room, closing the door.

Tootie took a deep breath. Then she tried her best to

wait patiently. It wasn't long before she heard the same urgent whispering from her parents as she had on previous nights. Tootie felt certain they were discussing something important, something which somehow was going to affect her in a drastic way.

Quietly, she got up and tiptoed across the room. After gently grasping the doorknob, she began slowly opening the door. She was just about to crouch low and listen when all of a sudden the hinge squeaked.

"Who's up?" Father asked.

For a second, Tootie didn't answer. But when she heard Father coming she quickly said, "It's me. I need to go to the bathroom."

"Hurry up, lass. It's late! Eve thought you were already asleep."

"I'm hurrying," Tootie responded. She knew there would be no more eavesdropping tonight. She quickly ran to the bathroom and then back to her room, firmly closing the bedroom door.

Maybe Joey has some oil or grease or something like that in his parents' store, Tootie thought. *I'll ask tomorrow and try to fix that stupid hinge*. With these thoughts she drifted into a restless sleep.

Early the next morning, Tootie woke to another cold day. Immediately she noticed there was no smell of porridge or toast wafting through the house. After grabbing her faded robe and pulling on her green, knitted slippers, she ran to the kitchen. Father was standing there, already dressed for the day, trying his best to cut a loaf of bread. She couldn't help but notice how help-less he was when he tried doing something practical. *He's so smart when it comes to things like mathematics*, Tootie thought, *but he can't handle common stuff*.

"Morning," Tootie greeted, and went to help.

"Good morning, lass." Donald handed her the bread knife. "Your mother had another real bad bout during the night." He refused to say the words "vomit" or "throw up" because he thought they were crude. But Tootie knew exactly what Father meant.

"What do you think's wrong with Mother?" Tootie asked. It seemed as though she'd asked that question at least a hundred times. There was just never an answer.

"I have my suspicions," Father said, and his voice sounded sad. "As a matter of fact, I want Eve to see a doctor tomorrow. I'm making the appointment for her. Since Dr. Jenkins moved, we've been in a quandary about whom to consult."

Tootie's heart pounded as she got out the double boiler to make the porridge. While measuring oats she asked, "Do you think Mama's going to die?"

"No, Tootie, now why would you ask a thing like that? She's just sick." Father smoothed his black hair with its three waves to the side. His thin face looked strained. "I not only want the doctor to look at Eve, I also want him to examine Buddy."

Tootie felt a shock run through her thin body. "Buddy? Why? He doesn't have a cold or anything."

"You ask too many questions," Father said and leaned

against the counter. "You know as well as anybody that Buddy is different. All of us have sort of ignored his slowness and simply put up with it, hoping someday he'd improve." Father shifted his weight and sighed deeply. "Well, he's eight years old, and it's high time we find out what makes him so . . . so . . . oh, you know."

It seemed as though her whole world were falling apart. She must have looked pathetic because Father put his arm around her narrow shoulders and whispered, "Cheer up, lass, it's just a doctor's appointment. In fact, I want you to go along tomorrow with them on the trolley. I need to stay here in the bakery, and your mother may need help. If she gets another one of her bouts on the bus. . . . Well, it would be better if you were there."

Tootie could see it now. She was holding onto Buddy with one hand, carrying the bucket in the other, and trying to comfort Mother as they bounced and swayed down Washington Street to the doctor. She did, however, feel a touch of pride that her father would trust her with such a grave responsibility.

"You're very grown-up for thirteen," Donald continued and then looked down at her small stature and smiled. "Your heart is as big as they come, lass. I thought of asking Pearl, but—" Without another word Father turned and left the kitchen.

Tears smarted in Tootie's hazel eyes, and her thin lips quivered. All of a sudden she felt like bawling. She and Father had never been so close. She stirred the cooking oats and swallowed hard, trying her best to keep back the tears. Finally she wiped the back of her sleeve across her eyes. *Maybe hard times do bring some good things*, she thought.

When the oatmeal was ready, she went into the bedroom to wake Pearl and Buddy. Buddy had wet his bed during the night and Tootie helped him change. Then she put the sheets in the bathtub and rinsed them out, hoping she'd have time to do the wash after school.

Pearl came back from the bathroom as Tootie was finishing dressing Buddy. "Tie that rope-belt tight," Pearl said. She was brushing through her black hair and parting it straight down the middle. "Daddy told me that Buddy's pants almost fell down yesterday in the bakery. That would have been awful! What will he do next to scare away customers?"

How could she say that in front of Buddy? Tootie gave her older sister a disgusted look, and then continued helping Buddy put on his socks and shoes. He was sitting on the edge of his bed while Tootie knelt in front of him. He reached out and began playing with her short brown curls. He giggled as her curls bounced up and down.

Tootie playfully shook her head at her brother and reached up to muss his hair. Buddy fell back onto the bed giggling. *It takes so little to make him happy*, Tootie thought. *I just wish he didn't have to spend all day down in the bakery with grouchy customers.* "Come on," Tootie said with a catch in her throat. "I made you some good, hot porridge."

After breakfast, Tootie rechecked her mother, making sure a bucket, a glass of water, and a fresh towel were handy. "Father says he wants you to see a doctor," Tootie whispered as she wiped her mother's forehead.

Eve nodded and attempted a smile.

Tootie decided not to mention anything about the comment concerning also having Buddy checked.

"Everything's going to be all right," Eve said. "Don't frown so. This is the time to trust God."

"Yes, Mama," Tootie said, wishing with all her might that she could learn to do just that.

"I hear Pearl calling for you," Eve continued. "You don't want to be late for school. I will be fine."

Tootie kissed her mother and hurried out of the bedroom. She grabbed two slices of bread for lunch and ran out of the apartment after Pearl. Father had already taken Buddy to the bakery.

"Good m-morning," Joey greeted, and tipped his hat. He had been leaning against the front door of the McCarthy's pie shop, waiting for them so they could walk to school together. "At your s-service," he said to Tootie and Pearl and then bowed low. He wore his black-and-white plaid jacket and baggy trousers. And, as always, his suspenders were twisted.

"You're a nut, Joey Staddler!" Tootie laughed.

"Now that's the truth!" Pearl agreed. Turning abruptly, she pulled up the collar of her old coat against the cold February morning and marched ahead of them down the boardwalk along Washington Street.

Joey looked at Tootie and shrugged. "What's the m-matter with her? Did she p-pin her hair too tight?"

"Shush!" Tootie giggled and tied her red scarf under her chin. "I need to hurry this morning because I have to tell Miss Penick I'm going to be absent tomorrow."

"What's up?"

"Oh, you know my mother's been sick. Well, I'm going with her to see the doctor." She purposefully didn't mention that they were also going to take Buddy. She could trust Joey—it wasn't that. Somehow she just didn't want to mention it.

The minute they reached the schoolgrounds, they spotted Irene and a group of girls gossiping by the front steps. The girls looked their way, and then Irene leaned into her circle of friends and whispered something more.

The entire group gasped.

Just as Tootie was about to pass them, Irene grabbed her arm and said, "I don't like the way your father talked to my mother."

Tootie pulled away as burning anger filled her body. "And I don't like the way your mother talks to my father or my little brother. In fact, your mother is rude! She'd better not come into our bakery ever again!"

Irene's face turned as pale as her off-white wool coat. "I'd like you to know that my mother was in hysterics last night when she came home. She was horrified by how that dumb brother of yours splattered apple pie all over her favorite fur! Your brother's a *retard*!"

Several girls in the circle giggled.

Irene continued with a real note of contempt in her voice, "And that father of yours isn't much better."

Tootie threw her books on the ground and her whole

body stiffened. "You're going to eat those words," she said through clenched teeth.

"You s-sure are!" Joey added and threw his books next to Tootie's. Then he put up his fists as if he and Tootie were about to fight a gang of street boys instead of a blond smart-mouthed girl.

Just then Miss Penick marched out of the school and down the steps toward them. "Enough!" she shouted. "We'll have none of that at Logan School."

"Did you see how they were going to attack me?" Irene began.

Miss Penick frowned. "Irene! That will be quite enough! All of us heard your comments."

Irene flipped her hair back, lifted her chin, and hurried up the steps into the school. The entire crowd of girls followed.

"It was all Irene's f-fault," Joey began.

Miss Penick's long, bird-like nose turned red with anger. "I doubt it, Joey Staddler. I doubt that very much! Ever since you teamed up with Tootie McCarthy, you've both become the troublemakers of this school. I never know what to expect next from you two."

Tootie and Joey stared in disbelief at each other and then back at their teacher.

"But—" Tootie began.

"No buts!" Miss Penick interrupted. "Irene and her mother are not the only ones with complaints against that brother of yours. He upsets everyone who comes to your parents' store. I'm surprised they're still in business. They'd be wise to lock him away!" Miss Penick turned and reentered the building.

Tootie didn't trust herself to say a word. *How can anybody be so cruel?*

The tardy bell rang, but still Tootie and Joey stood at the bottom step. Everyone else had gone inside. Finally Joey picked up their books and handed Tootie hers. She grabbed them, purposefully held her head high, and marched into school.

Early the next morning, Tootie woke to the smell of buttermilk pancakes. After bounding out of bed and scurrying down the hallway, she was completely surprised. There stood Mother by the gas stove flipping pancakes and humming, "The Old Rugged Cross."

"Mama, you're better!" Tootie cried and ran to her side. "God really does answer prayer!"

Eve smiled. "You know he does, lass, one way or the other." She handed Tootie the pancake turner. "Here, finish these for me so I can set table."

While Mother was taking out a stack of plates from the cupboard, she continued. "Honestly, Tootie, don't get your hopes too high. At least, not just yet. I'm still feeling rather sick. This nausea comes and goes." Then she nodded toward the pancakes. "I just thought we might like something special before we head out to see the doctor."

"Oh," is all Tootie could say, and her disappointment showed in her face and voice. She pushed a few curls away from her eyes and slowly began pouring more batter onto the hot skillet. "Do you really think we still need to see the doctor?"

"Yes, lass, I do." Mother's voice sounded definite. "It's not for me, so much. It's for our Buddy. We've always talked about taking him to be examined, but I guess we've been too scared. We've sort of been afraid to hear that there is no hope for improvement."

Tootie knew that feeling.

Mother began placing knives and forks. "Maybe it's not too late though. Maybe the doctor *can* help Buddy. As for me . . . I truly think this is just a bad case of the flu."

"Really?"

"Yes, dear. Now quit your worrying."

About an hour later, Pearl left for school, and Father went down to the bakery to help Mrs. Roseen, the baker. Much to Mrs. Roseen's irritation, Father never actually rolled up his sleeves and worked. Instead, he mainly visited with customers, ordered supplies, and kept the books. When Mother was well and could help in the bakery, she always worked alongside Mrs. Roseen and, as a result, the tension eased. But since Eve had been sick for the past months, Mrs. Roseen was always on the verge of quitting.

Tootie kept mulling over these thoughts as she helped Buddy dress in his brown corduroy knickerbockers and heavy wool socks.

Mother had packed syrup sandwiches for Tootie and Buddy, and they were putting on their coats when the doorbell rang. To their surprise, it was Pastor Myers.

"Good morning," Mother greeted.

The young pastor from the Alliance Bible Church smiled, "Good morning, Mrs. McCarthy. I'm glad I caught you before you left." Then he nodded toward Tootie and Buddy. "I was just going into the church a few minutes ago when Joey Staddler dropped by on his way to school. He mentioned you had a doctor's appointment sometime today."

"That's right," Eve replied, somewhat surprised. "As a matter of fact, that's where we're heading right now. Our appointment is for nine o'clock."

"I would be happy to take you," he offered. He turned and pointed down to the curb in front of the bakery. "As you know, the elders of our church have given me the use of that Model T. It's in fair condition." Then chuckling, he added, "With a lot of prayer, I think it just might get us to the doctor and back."

Eve smiled. "We would really appreciate a ride."

Tootie felt such relief. The last thing she wanted to do was to take the trolley at this time of the morning. It was always so crowded. Besides, she was certain Mother's stomach was feeling queasy from the pancakes.

"I like your Model T," Tootie said with genuine excitement.

"T . . . T . . . T . . . T . . . T," Buddy sang while clapping his hands.

Pastor Myers looked tenderly at Buddy and patted him on the shoulder. "Come on, young man. Let's show these ladies to the automobile."

Mother sat next to Pastor Myers as he drove down

Washington Street and then into the high-class business section of town. But she held the small bucket in her lap the entire trip. As they pulled up by the curb, Mother vomited. Pastor Myers didn't seem to mind. He jumped out of the car and came around to open the door. "How long do you think you'll be?" he asked.

Eve looked embarrassed as she wiped her mouth and laid the hand towel over the top of the bucket. "I don't know. It could be quite some time. But whatever you do, don't wait. We'll take the trolley home when we're finished."

Pastor Myers didn't respond as he helped them out of the Model T. Then he said, "There are plenty of errands for me to do while I'm in this area. Besides, several of my church flock live close by and I'm sure it's time for a visit. I should be back in about an hour and a half, maybe two. I'll be waiting right here for you."

"Thank you," Mother said and gently squeezed Pastor Myers' hand. Then she turned quickly and led the way into the building.

At exactly nine o'clock a stern-looking nurse stepped into the waiting room and announced, "Next!" The receptionist handed the nurse a chart and nodded toward the McCarthys.

Before Tootie could stop him, Buddy jumped to his feet and, as always, mimicked what he heard. "Next!" he said in the same sharp tone. Several in the waiting room began snickering.

The nurse glared at Buddy as if personally offended. "Well," she said and slapped the chart against the palm of her hand. "Impertinence from an . . ." she scanned the chart and continued, "from an eight-year-old."

Once again Buddy simply repeated what he heard, "Old . . . old . . ."

"Hush," Mother interrupted and shifted the bucket. The putrid smell came through the towel and filled the room.

"Follow me," the nurse said abruptly. "Dr. Dunn will see you in his office." The nurse marched down the narrow hallway, and the three McCarthys followed.

The moment they entered, Dr. Dunn stood to his feet and motioned for them to sit in the comfortable chairs directly in front of his desk. The walls of his office were covered with dozens of framed photographs of a large white house and numerous diplomas. But Tootie didn't take time to look too closely because her eyes were drawn to the doctor, who had a big barrel-shaped chest that tapered down into a narrow waist. His hair was reddish-blond and was cut so short that it was no more than a quarter of an inch long. It stuck out all over his scalp and reminded Tootie of peach fuzz. Even his eyebrows and eyelashes had the same pinkish, peach fuzz appearance. His face looked puffy and there were dark circles under his eyes, as though he hadn't slept in days. As the doctor sat down in his swivel chair, the nurse placed the chart in front of him. Then she took the bucket and left.

"When your husband called, Mrs. McCarthy," Dr. Dunn began, "he explained your symptoms to me. I will, of course, need to examine you later. But for now, I merely want to get acquainted."

Eve nodded nervously.

Then the doctor stared for a moment at Buddy, who was sitting on the opposite side of Tootie. "Mr. McCarthy also mentioned your son. Later, I may want to examine this boy."

"Boy . . . boy . . . boy," Buddy repeated and swung his feet.

"Yes," the doctor said and his serious expression never changed. "I may want to examine you, boy. But I've already assessed the situation."

What in the world does that mean? Tootie thought. She stared at Dr. Dunn, who appeared to be about the same age as his grumpy nurse. Suddenly Tootie noticed that Dr. Dunn was staring back.

"I didn't realize I had three patients to examine this morning," he said.

"This is one of our daughters," Mother explained. "She's not sick. She's just come to help."

"Fine . . . fine," the doctor said. And then for the first time he changed his expression and smiled benevolently at the three in front of him. Tootie didn't like his smile. Somehow it never reached his small eyes which seemed almost hidden behind all that peach fuzz.

But Mother obviously didn't have any reservations about the man because she answered his questions freely. She told him how long she had been sick and how terrible the stomach cramps became when she vomited. It was evident the doctor felt he was onto something when he asked, "Think back over your most recent episodes. What preceded each incident? Let's see if a pattern emerges. If there is a pattern, we'll have to remove whatever is disturbing you. I honestly think, thus far, that a lot of your problem is emotional."

Tootie didn't exactly know what that meant. She sat up straight in her chair and scooted to the edge so she could plant her feet squarely on the floor. Leaning slightly forward, she listened intently to every word Mother said. Before long, even Tootie started to see what the doctor meant by a pattern. Mother got sick over basically two things: the failing bakery business and Buddy's constant need for attention.

Dr. Dunn took page after page of notes. Every once in a while he would glance over at Buddy who was rubbing the corduroy material between his fingers. Finally Buddy quit rubbing his trousers and began playing with his tongue. The doctor shook his head and then continued taking notes.

It wasn't long before Dr. Dunn dropped his pen on the medical chart and stared at Mother. "You poor woman," he said, "you've put up with far too much! You have been living under such distressing circumstances that your body is literally giving up. If we don't do something immediately, you may not survive."

Both Eve and Tootie stared at the doctor in disbelief.

Tootie almost fell off the edge of her chair and tears smarted her eyes. "Is Mama going to die?"

"Die . . . Die . . . Die," Buddy repeated.

Dr. Dunn ignored him and addressed Tootie, "Your

mother may die if drastic changes aren't made. And I mean drastic!"

"Good gracious, Doctor," Eve interrupted, "I'm sure I'm not that bad. What in the world are you talking about?"

"After a thorough examination, I am confident I'll find much evidence that the pressure you have been living under during these past years is taking its toll. You probably have peptic ulcers and you may have colitis. I wouldn't be surprised if your condition is even worse than that."

"Can't you give my mother some medicine to make her better?" Tootie asked. "I'm sure there is *something* you can do."

Dr. Dunn's fair complexion turned as red as his hair and brows. "Young lady, I intend to prescribe medication for your mother. But that won't be enough. What I am about to suggest will shock you. It may even make you mad."

And then he turned in his swivel chair and addressed Mother. "Remember, Evelyn McCarthy, what I am about to say is for your own peace of mind."

Mother grabbed Tootie's hand, and Tootie squeezed back. Then Tootie reached over to hold Buddy's hand, but he wasn't paying any attention. He had pulled his feet up onto the office chair and was fiddling with his shoes, mumbling, "Catch . . . catch . . . catch." Tootie knew that even if he had been listening, he wouldn't have understood the conversation.

"Well," Dr. Dunn began and cleared his throat. He

got up, walked over to the window, and said matter-of-factly, "I own a large place outside of town. I opened a home several years ago, just for cases like yours. It's a good place, and I know it will help your situation."

Mother frowned. "What are you suggesting?"

The doctor didn't answer. He kept looking out the window.

Tootie scooted closer to Mother. She had this awful feeling that Dr. Dunn wanted Mother to move away from home and live in the country. How could they survive without her?

Eve must have been thinking the same thing because she said, "You don't understand. I couldn't possibly leave my family at a time like this. I'm needed. Our pie business is failing, and Donald can't keep it running on his own. I just want to get some medication and get better so I can help. That's all. Moving to some country retreat isn't the answer. It's totally out of the question."

Tootie felt such relief. She hadn't noticed that Buddy had left his chair and was playing with some instruments over in the corner.

Just then Dr. Dunn turned away from the window and looked straight at them. "I didn't mean you, Mrs. McCarthy. Of course I realize you can't up and leave. I meant him," and he pointed to Buddy who had a stethoscope dangling from his hands.

"Buddy?" both Mother and Tootie shouted in surprise.

Buddy jumped and dropped the doctor's stethoscope. Slowly his brown corduroy knickerbockers turned all dark in front. Tootie knew he was wetting his pants.

Mother got to her feet. "I believe I've misunderstood you," she said. "Are you suggesting that we move our Buddy to this home in the country?"

"By all means! This is 1928. It's not like we're back in the Dark Ages. Surely you've heard of asylums? Most people who have children like him put them away. There's no hope for improvement for him, or for you, Mrs. McCarthy, if you don't make some drastic changes. Besides, it's healthier for all involved when the feeble-minded are put together. Believe me, they prefer living with their own kind in an asylum."

"No!" Tootie gasped. "My Buddy Boy is *not* going to any asylum! They're for crazy people. My brother is *not* crazy and he's *not* going to be locked up!"

Buddy began crying. Tootie knew he didn't understand everything that was being said, but was reacting to all the tension.

"Calm down, young lady," Dr. Dunn said in a stern tone. "Can't you see that you're upsetting both your brother and your mother? Besides, Fairbolt is different from any other place you've heard about. We care about our inmates. It's not like some of those dreadful places you've read about in the newspaper."

Tootie hadn't read any such articles.

"Catch . . . catch . . . catch," Buddy said through his tears. Tootie knew that was his way of expressing he was upset and wanted to leave.

"You will be able to play catch with other boys, if you move out to Fairbolt," Dr. Dunn announced proudly. "We take care of boys like you."

Eve smoothed a few strands of graying hair back to her bun. Then she pursed her thin lips. Finally she said, "Lass, will you take Buddy outside and wait for me? There are a few things I want to discuss with the doctor."

Tootie went ice cold. *What's she going to do? Mother would never allow Buddy to move away from home, would she?* With great agitation, Tootie took Buddy by the hand and led him out of Dr. Dunn's office.

From the moment Eve got into Pastor Myers's Model T, it was obvious she was feeling better. She held the freshly washed bucket, which was now stuffed to overflowing with brochures about Fairbolt, to her chest. Then she set the bucket on the floor by her feet and said, "Thank you for coming, Pastor. I hope you haven't waited long."

"No, as a matter of fact, I just arrived." He quickly got out of the car and went to the front to crank up the engine. Then he hollered over the noise, "These two were already waiting for me when I got here." After getting back into the automobile, he glanced at Tootie and Buddy who were huddled together in the back seat. Buddy had his head resting on Tootie's bony shoulder, and he looked miserable. "I haven't been able to get a word out of either one of them," Pastor Myers said gently. "Hope everything's all right."

Mother didn't answer directly, but she turned and said over her shoulder, "Don't worry, lass, or you either, laddy," she said. "We're not going to make any snap decision about Fairbolt. We'll discuss all this as a family."

What's there to discuss, Tootie thought rebelliously. *My brother isn't going to be sent away to any asylum.* Tootie watched Pastor Myers's big hands as they grasped the wheel and steered out into the traffic. Every once in a while he glanced into the rearview mirror and smiled encouragingly. Then she saw him look down at the bucket of brochures and frown. *I wonder if he knows anything about asylums,* Tootie thought. But she certainly didn't want to ask because she didn't want to admit, even to herself, that Fairbolt was being considered.

Later that night after supper and the dishes, Tootie helped Buddy get ready for bed. He wanted to wear his favorite faded blue pajamas with holes. The holes were caused by constant rubbing of the soft material. "Ahhh," he moaned contentedly.

Tootie could hear snatches of conversation coming from the other room. The brochures were spread out on the table, and Mother was reading the information to Father and Pearl. Tootie noticed that her mother was already looking and sounding stronger since seeing the doctor, sort of like she had renewed hope that things would somehow improve.

"Fairbolt looks beautiful!" Pearl said, staring down at a picture on the front of one the pamphlets. "I'd love to live in a big house like that. How often can we visit?"

"Nothing's definite, lass," Mother cautioned. "We're

simply going to discuss this matter calmly and logically."
Then Mother's voice sank to barely more than a whisper. It was hard for Tootie to hear, but it sounded as though Mother said, "To be honest, I don't think I could bear sending my son away. No one could love him as much as we do."

"I'd miss him, too," Pearl admitted. "Life just wouldn't be the same without Buddy. I don't want him to go. I don't even think we should talk about it." And then Pearl suddenly started to giggle, "But I certainly wouldn't miss his awful snoring; he keeps me awake every night. By the way, is this Fairbolt place expensive?"

"Yes," Eve admitted. "We'd have to take out a loan."

"But I'm sure the bank will give us one," Father said. His tone sounded incredibly sad. "They'll want the bakery as security, or collateral, or whatever they call it."

Mother added, "And this brochure says that Dr. Dunn wants the entire payment in advance."

"If we do get a loan, can I get my front teeth fixed? I hate them so much! Oh, please!" Pearl pleaded.

"Wait a minute," Father interrupted. "Not so fast. We're not talking about teeth, Pearl, we're talking about Fairbolt—and Buddy—and the bakery. Remember? Let's take one thing at a time. Besides Tootie isn't even here to discuss this matter. Let's wait until she comes.

"By the way, we've got to be cautious about these kinds of places. Just last week I read in *The Tribune* . . ."

Tootie quickly shut the bedroom door. She tried her best to put on a smile as she turned toward Buddy. Her chest felt like someone was jumping on it and her head throbbed.

But Buddy seemed happy and content as he lay in bed. He was exhausted from his outing. He smiled up at her, unaware of the importance of the discussion taking place in the other room or of the decision ahead.

Tootie tucked him in and then knelt. "How about saying prayers with me?"

Buddy folded his hands and closed his eyes. He moved his head back and forth on the pillow and kept saying reverently, "God . . . God . . . God."

Tears slowly rolled down Tootie's cheeks. Buddy always had a genuine closeness to God, more than anyone she knew. He somehow worshiped the Almighty as if he could truly communicate with Him. Tootie stared at her brother as his lips moved silently. He must be talking to God in his own private way, she thought.

Please, God, Tootie prayed silently. *You know Buddy doesn't understand what's going on. Please don't allow him to be put into Fairbolt. I couldn't stand it. Please let him stay here with me. And please heal Mother another way, without sending Buddy to an asylum.*

Suddenly she felt fingers in her curls. Buddy whispered, "Toot . . . Toot."

"Oh, Buddy Boy," Tootie whispered back. Her voice choked with emotion.

Buddy patted her awkwardly, "Toot . . . Toot . . . Toot," he said again, looking at her with complete admiration and trust. Then he yawned and stretched out in bed. It wasn't long before he was sound asleep, with his snores getting louder and louder.

When Tootie finally joined the family, she heard Mother explaining, "Yes, I had a brief exam. Dr. Dunn said my health is terrible. I guess this pressure is getting to be too much for me. He honestly doesn't know how much more I can take. He says I need a complete rest, and that having Buddy away for a while would help."

"Did this doctor examine Buddy?" Father asked.

"No," Tootie interrupted. "He hardly looked at him."

"Tootie's right," Eve said and smiled gently. "Come and sit down, dear." Then Mother continued, "Dr. Dunn told me that he didn't need to examine Buddy right away. He explained that if we put him in Fairbolt, he'll have a complete examination and good medical care. He also said it was obvious that Buddy has something called mongolism. I think he called him a Mongoloid." Then Mother started crying.

"It's all right, Eve," Father said and put his arm around her. "Come on . . . what else did this doctor say?"

Eve began wiping her eyes and finally she blew her nose. "The doctor said Buddy would never be normal—not *ever!*"

"Why would he say a thing like that?" Tootie shouted. "How does he know? And I don't like him calling my brother names."

"Lower your voice," Father said. "Can't you tell this is hard on all of us? And this doctor wasn't calling Buddy any bad names. Mongolism is a mental condition. I've read about it. It's something you're born with. It means your brain isn't completely normal. And I think we've sort of suspected that all along."

Tootie burst into tears. "I can't stand this! Nobody's taking my brother away from me!" She turned and ran into the bathroom, slamming the door behind her.

First thing the next morning, Father announced, "I've come to a decision. We're closing the bakery today and we're all taking a trip out to Fairbolt. I've read the brochures. And I know how to get there. We'll make a surprise visit—totally unannounced and uninvited. That way we can judge the place for ourselves."

"I don't want to go," Tootie said.

"I knew you'd say that," Father responded. "But I want you to come, lass. You see, I want to take Buddy so we know his reaction to the place. He'll do better with you along."

Tootie put her hands on her hips. "I don't see why that's important. He's *not* going to stay there!"

"Tootie!" Eve said. "Don't talk to your father in such a manner."

Tootie tried calming her voice, but she kept her hands on her hips. "I at least want Joey to come. He's good with Buddy, too."

Just then Mother hurried into the bathroom. They could all hear her being violently sick to her stomach.

Donald looked around at his daughters with a worried expression. "I'll go ask Pastor Myers for the use of his Model T. Tootie, you go ask the Staddlers about

Joey. I don't know if they can spare him on a Saturday, but you can try. Pearl, you get Buddy ready."

Soon they were all piled in the Model T. Mother and Father sat in the front, while Pearl, Buddy, Joey, and Tootie were crowded into the back seat.

Buddy was so excited about another ride in the car that he kept bouncing and yelling, "Weeee!"

Pearl tried to crowd closer to her side of the automobile. "I hate feeling so mussed," she mumbled. "Quit jumping on my dress, Buddy. You're wrinkling it."

While all this was going on, Tootie began anxiously explaining to Joey the events of the past few days. "Dr. Dunn says Mother needs complete rest from taking care of Buddy. He says Buddy should go to a place called Fairbolt . . . for his own good and for Mother's."

"What kind of place is F-Fairbolt?" Joey whispered.

Tootie could hardly get out the word. She swallowed hard and then mouthed, "an asylum."

Joey gulped.

"We've got to look around the place," Tootie said in a barely audible tone, with tears stinging her eyes. "We've just got to find something that will stop my parents from sending Buddy there."

At first, Joey didn't say a word. He brushed his straight brown hair back from his eyes. Then he leaned across Tootie and said to Buddy, "Weeee! Weeee!" He too started bouncing and continuing to say, "Weeee!" until Buddy began to giggle. Finally Joey looked at Tootie and whispered, "We'll f-find something wrong with that place. We're not l-letting him go to any insane asylum!"

To everyone's surprise, Fairbolt was locked behind an eight-foot gate. The house was the same one pictured on the brochures, and the morning sun framed the white-columned estate in bright sunlight. Curtains were drawn at every window which was not surprising because it was still early. Except for the locked gate, the place looked inviting.

Father got out of the car and fiddled with the lock. Finally he yelled, "Hey, is anyone home?"

Just then Dr. Dunn came out of Fairbolt's front door and waved. "I'll get the key," he called back and disappeared into the house.

"What's going on?" Tootie asked suspiciously. "Why would they lock the gate?"

Father explained that it was probably a precaution. He didn't seem upset about the locked gate and neither did Mother. They nodded at each other as though locked gates were a real plus.

Tootie and Joey got out of the car to look around.

"Don't go far," Father said. "I'm sure the good doctor will be here shortly."

"Good doctor," Tootie mouthed and made a face.

The thick branches of a huge crab apple tree inside the property hung over the fence. Joey jumped and tried grabbing for a branch. "This would m-make a good climbing tree if I could jump that high. Wonder if the c-crab apples will be any good in the Spring?"

Tootie stomped her foot. "Joey Staddler! We're not here to talk about crab apples. Buddy's life is at stake!"

Just then the barrel-chested Dr. Dunn arrived with a

batch of keys in his hands. He smiled in his benevolent fashion, which increased Tootie's irritation. But everyone else in her family seemed quite taken by the man. Pearl even whispered loudly that she loved the doctor's red hair. After he unlocked the gate, he came over to the car and made a special point of talking with Buddy. He reached his hand into the back seat, saying, "Welcome, young man."

Buddy repeated, "Man . . . man . . . man."

Everyone laughed—all except Tootie and Joey.

After the rest of the introductions, Dr. Dunn pointed to a place where Father could park the car. He explained that no one was generally allowed to visit Fairbolt unannounced. "However," he said with a smile, "we'll overlook it just this once. I find that anything unexpected disturbs our inmates unduly. We hold to quite a schedule, and I'm very protective of my little friends." Once again Dr. Dunn patted Buddy on the back.

This upset Tootie even further, but the rest of the family appeared to like the gesture. Also, she hated the word *inmate*. *What in the world is an inmate? Sounds like a prisoner*. Again she stared at the white mansion with its drawn curtains.

Dr. Dunn led them up the broad steps to the huge front porch. They passed two gigantic white columns, each bigger than the trunk of the crab apple tree. The porch seemed to wrap around the front of the home, and it held at least a dozen urns filled with miniature trees.

"It's beautiful!" Pearl whispered to Tootie. "I wish we could live here."

Tootie preferred their small apartment above the bakery. *Any place where we can be together as a family is better than this,* she thought.

Dr. Dunn opened the elegantly carved double doors with a flourish and ushered them into the foyer. Standing in the middle of the entrance room, with her arms folded across her ample bosom, was the stern nurse from his office. She wore a white uniform over her firm, broad figure and a nurse's cap pinned to her tightly permed hair.

"Welcome to Fairbolt," she said.

Tootie didn't think her voice sounded one bit welcoming.

The nurse continued, "If we had known you were coming, we would have been better prepared for you."

"I've already chided them," the doctor said with a shake of his head. "Please allow me to introduce Miss Bonzer. She's our head nurse here at Fairbolt. And as you are aware, sometimes she assists me at my office in town."

Suddenly a young, normal-looking boy, who appeared to be about Buddy's age, came into the foyer with a ball in his hands.

Tootie had a strange feeling. It was as though this boy had come on stage after being cued by the director. He came right up to Buddy and said, "Want to play?"

Buddy squealed with delight. "Catch . . . catch . . . catch," he said and grabbed the ball from the boy.

"See," Dr. Dunn said as he looked at the McCarthy family, "your son is already feeling at home. This other little fellow is one of our inmates. His name is Charles. Doesn't he look happy and healthy?"

Tootie saw her parents nod their approval. Father reached over and tenderly put his arm around Mother's shoulder. "Everything's going to be fine." He spoke in low tones. "This is a good place for our son. He'll even have friends his own age to play with."

Tears ran down Mother's pale cheeks.

Donald continued, "Then you can concentrate on getting better. We need to give this place serious consideration."

It felt as if a hot knife cut into Tootie's heart. *No!* she wanted to scream. *I'll play catch with Buddy after school. He doesn't have to move all the way out here to Fairbolt to play ball and have some fun.* But Tootie knew no one would listen. Even Joey appeared to approve of Fairbolt as he hurried outside to play catch with the two boys.

What am I going to do? Tootie thought. *Oh, God, what am I going to do?*

On the way home from Fairbolt, Buddy kept bouncing in the back seat saying excitedly, "Carls . . . catch . . . Carls . . . catch."

"Hush, lad, that's enough," Father scolded. "Besides, that boy's name is Charles, not 'Carls.' I'm glad you had such a good time. But now we're trying to talk, and we can't hear ourselves think with all that commotion you're making."

"Carls . . . catch?" Buddy said again, but this time he whispered it right into Tootie's ear. Then he nestled close and laid his small round head in the crook of Tootie's neck. "Carls . . . catch?" he whispered again.

Tears stung Tootie's eyes. She glanced across Buddy at Pearl. The wind was blowing through the open Model T and Pearl was trying desperately to keep her hair in place. She kept rearranging the hairpins in her coiled buns. Tootie felt like grabbing the stupid pins and throwing them out of the Model T.

Then she looked to her left where Joey was fiddling with the softball that Charles had given him. He was

49

staring at the ball and rolling it round and round in his hands. Tootie had all she could do not to snatch the ball and throw it out of the automobile after Pearl's hairpins.

Frantically she began rubbing and patting Buddy's head as it rested on her shoulder. She watched Mother lean close to Father in the front seat. "Wasn't that little room Nurse Bonzer showed us nice and clean?"

Donald agreed. "And Dr. Dunn assured me that Buddy wouldn't have to stay long. He says with Buddy gone, you'll have time to rest and you'll get better real soon."

Eve sighed.

Father continued, "Buddy will be taken care of properly."

"Properly" should mean being with your own family! Tootie thought. She rubbed Buddy even harder.

Buddy became tired of Tootie's frantic rubbing. He pulled away, complaining, "Toot . . . Toot!"

Mother glanced over her shoulder and frowned. Then she leaned closer to Father and continued talking.

The moment they drove up in front of the McCarthy's pie shop, Joey jumped out onto the boardwalk and handed the softball to Buddy. Mother, Pearl, and Buddy hurried up to the apartment while Father drove the Model T back to Pastor Myers. Tootie just stood with her arms folded across her flat chest and a scowl almost shading her hazel eyes.

"I-I want to talk," Joey said.

Tootie's scowl became deeper. "What's there to say?

It seems to me you could've helped by not having so much fun playing catch with that Charles boy!"

"B-but, Tootie. Let me explain."

"No!" Tootie turned and dashed up to the apartment, slamming the door.

The rest of the day Mother spent in bed. She vomited at least six times and Pearl and Tootie took turns tending to her. Buddy kept wanting to play catch and he ended up crying uncontrollably. Even Tootie couldn't calm him. Father spread out the bakery's financial books across the cherrywood table in the dining area and worked well into the night.

The entire family stayed home from church the next morning and Tootie didn't see Joey all day. She was still mad at him because she thought he went along with the whole Fairbolt idea.

By Monday morning Tootie's temper was ready to explode. Father had said that he and Mother were going to take a week to come to a final decision about Fairbolt. "We don't want to put Buddy at any asylum no matter how nice a place it might be," he explained before she and Pearl left for school. "Fairbolt will be our last resort. But if Eve doesn't improve . . . and Buddy has to stay with me in the bakery upsetting customers, well—"

Tootie dashed out of the apartment not wanting to hear anymore. She ignored Joey and hurried to school. While rushing down the hallway, Irene stopped her. "How's that retard brother of yours?" Irene teased.

Tootie shoved past her so hard she knocked Irene into the wall. Irene gasped for breath and backed away.

"I-I feel like doing that t-to that boy, Charles." Joey said. He had come up alongside Tootie.

"What?" Tootie stopped and stared. "You were all chummy with him."

"I-I didn't trust him. He's up t-to no good!"

"Really? How do you know?" Tootie asked.

"Something's s-suspicious is going on out at that F-Fairbolt place and Ch-Charles is in on it."

"He's only eight or nine," Tootie said, still astounded at her friend. Then she added, "Oh, Joey, I hate that place. I just *hate* it!"

"Me, too," Joey said. "And I heard your d-dad say it will cost three thousand dollars to p-put Buddy there."

"My folks can't afford that!" Tootie said.

Irene passed with her friends. "My folks can't afford that!" she mimicked. The other girls laughed.

Joey had to hold Tootie back. When she tried to pull away, she noticed Principal Harris and Miss Penick coming toward them.

"To your classrooms," Mr. Harris demanded. "We'll have no fighting in my school." He frowned at Tootie and Joey. So did Miss Penick.

Everyone scattered to their respective rooms.

The following days seemed to go by in a haze. There was school, plus all the homework. Tootie was afraid her grades were going down, down, down, especially in mathematics. Irene was continuing to spread rumors, and Tootie could feel her own temper constantly on the verge of exploding. Besides all this, there was work to do in the bakery every day after school, and piles upon piles of dirty clothes. Mother got increasingly sicker and had to spend the entire week in bed.

Early Saturday morning, Father came into the bedroom and shook Tootie and Pearl. "Up, lasses," he whispered. "I want you to come with me."

Tootie didn't even take time to grab her robe. "What's the matter?" she asked as she scrambled out of bed.

"Hush," Donald said. "I don't want to wake Buddy."

When they got to the living room, Mother was lying on the sofa. She looked weak and her eyes were framed in dark circles. Tears began streaming down her cheeks as Tootie and Pearl rushed to her side.

"What's happening?" Tootie cried.

"You look awful, Mother!" Pearl added.

Eve grasped her daughters' hands and said, "Sit down. Your father wants to tell you of our decision."

Tootie plopped on the floor in front of the sofa with a feeling of doom settling over her. Pearl finished putting on her bathrobe and then hurried to the overstuffed floral chair.

"It's like this," Father began as he paced the floor. He too was in his bathrobe and his black hair, which was usually combed neatly into three beautiful waves, was hanging haphazardly across his forehead. "Your mother and I have been doing a lot of thinking. This has been an extremely difficult time in all of our lives." He ran his fingers through his hair several times, then stopped in front of the old dark-oak piano with the word *Miester* written in gold above middle C. Very lightly he moved his index finger over the dusty keys.

The sound sent renewed chills through Tootie's shivering body.

Mother reached over and touched Tootie's arm. Then she took off one of her blankets and handed it to Tootie.

Father waited until everyone was settled. "Eve and I have decided to take out a loan against the bakery." Once again he ran his fingers along the keys of the old, out-of-tune piano. Then he turned and faced them. "Eve and I have come to the conclusion that we have no other choice. We are going to take Buddy, our little laddy-boy, out to Fairbolt today and admit him."

"No!" Tootie gasped. "We can't!" She burst into tears. "*Please*—please don't!"

"We've thought this over," Father said. His voice didn't sound angry, just sad and defeated. "Here is the check. After much discussion with the bank, we've finally received this loan against our bakery." Father picked up a piece of paper from the top of the upright piano and stared at it. His whole body seemed to sag.

No one dared breathe.

Donald sighed several times and then looked around at his family. "We have to pay in advance for an entire year at Fairbolt. That totals three thousand dollars!"

Tootie's head throbbed.

"However, your mother and I feel Buddy won't need to be away for a full year. We're sure that Eve will begin to get well just as soon as she can have some rest. Dr.

Dunn has assured us that if Mother is better and we want to bring Buddy back home before the year is finished, we will get a partial refund."

"No!" Tootie cried again. "What do you mean, a year?"

"We will be allowed to visit," Mother said and blew her nose. "Dr. Dunn says that all we have to do is call and make an appointment."

"An appointment to see my own brother?"

"I know it sounds awful, Tootie," Father admitted. "We don't like it any more than you do. But what else can we do?"

Tootie jumped to her feet and let the blanket fall to the floor around her thin ankles. "I can quit school. And so can Pearl. We can stay home and work."

"That's right," Pearl said.

But Tootie didn't think she sounded one bit convincing.

And then Pearl added, "By any chance do you think there'll be any money left over from the three thousand dollars to get my front teeth fixed?"

Everyone stared at Pearl.

Tootie couldn't believe her sister's selfishness.

Finally Mother said, "We know that your teeth are a big concern to you, Pearl. We wish with all our hearts that we could do something about them." Then Mother shrugged and a helpless look spread across her face. "But with this large amount for Fairbolt, and then payments for my medical care . . ."

"Like I said," Tootie interrupted, "I can quit school. I want to stay home and help."

"We won't allow that," Father said. "Besides, we've recently heard that all this upheaval at home is affecting your school work. Miss Penick came by the other day and talked with us."

"She makes me so mad!"

"Did any of my teachers come?" Pearl asked.

"Not yet," Mother added. "But they will if we don't do something real soon."

In the following discussion, it was decided that Pearl would not go with them to Fairbolt but stay and take care of Mother and also assist Mrs. Roseen in the bakery with the monthly cleaning. Tootie was supposed to pack for Buddy and then go with Father as he drove Buddy to Fairbolt. Upon Tootie's insistence, her parents agreed that Joey Staddler could come along, if his parents allowed.

If only the Gypsies were here, Tootie thought. *I'm sure Mara and Leon would think of something. Maybe Buddy could go and live with them in one of their caravans.* Tootie knew she was being totally unrealistic. She didn't even know where the Gypsies had moved.

With tears streaming down her face and dripping off her quivering chin, Tootie got up and walked into their bedroom. She waited for a few minutes by Buddy's bed. She didn't want him to wake and see her like that. Quickly she wiped her tears and tried to smile. Finally she said, "Wake up, Buddy Boy." She bent down and kissed him on the tip of his nose.

Buddy opened his almond-shaped eyes and smiled up at Tootie. Then he pushed his covers aside and grinned at his dry pajamas and sheets.

"Good boy!" Tootie said with all the love in her heart showing across her face.

Hurry, Buddy, go to the bathroom. And then come back and I'll help you dress." She stopped because the next words were hard to say. "We're—we're going on a trip."

Buddy frowned. It was obvious he didn't understand.

"Go see Charles," Tootie said.

"Carls . . . catch! Carls . . . catch!" Buddy said clapping his chubby hands.

"Yes," Tootie admitted, tousling his hair. "You are going to play catch with Charles." She wanted to explain that he would be staying, but she didn't know how.

While Buddy hurried to the bathroom, Tootie pulled the old tattered suitcase out from under her bed and dropped it onto the floor. Then she opened Buddy's bureau drawer and began taking things out. But when she reached the brown corduroy knickerbockers she put her finger through one of the holes, hoping that Dr. Dunn and Miss Bonzer wouldn't mind the way Buddy rubbed holes in his clothes. Once again she had to swallow hard to keep back the tears.

Then she grabbed one of his plaid flannel shirts and hugged it to her face. She knew she had to regain control before her brother returned. Finally she folded the shirt and placed it into the suitcase along with Buddy's other things.

As the McCarthys sat around the breakfast table, everyone was quiet—except Buddy. He kept saying, "Carls . . . catch! Carls . . . catch!"

Mother was drinking black tea and feeding Buddy large spoonfuls of oatmeal. Eve lovingly wiped his chin and dabbed at the corners of his mouth. Finally she said, "Don't talk while you're eating, lad. It's not polite." Then she mumbled, "I don't want you to get in trouble at . . . at your . . . at Fairbolt."

Not another word was said for the remainder of the meal. Tootie noticed that Pearl and Father looked miserable. She even thought she saw tears in their eyes. But she couldn't be sure because they kept their heads lowered, staring at their bowls of uneaten cereal.

The porridge felt as if it were piling up in Tootie's throat. The more she tried to swallow, the more choked she became. Finally Tootie dropped her spoon, shoved her chair away from the table, ran into the bedroom, and flung herself lengthways across her bed, sobbing bitterly.

About ten minutes later, Mother came into the bedroom. She shut and latched the suitcase. Tootie didn't look up from the bed because she was certain Mother was also crying. Pearl had come into the room and picked up the case.

"Why?" Tootie sobbed into the blanket after Pearl left.

"We've gone through all this, lass," Eve responded. "You know there's no other way. You'd better hurry if you're going. Father has returned with Pastor Myers's Model T, and the Staddlers have agreed that Joey can go. I know it will help to have him with you—especially on the ride back. He's waiting downstairs."

Numbly Tootie got up, put on her coat, and left the apartment. Buddy was already sitting next to Father in the front seat. He held the tattered suitcase in his lap and Charles's softball in his hands. He wore his coat and wool cap with the flaps that came down over his ears.

Tootie thought her little brother looked happy and excited as he squirmed impatiently. She also knew deep down in her heart that Buddy wouldn't understand when they left him at Fairbolt. He would feel alone, lost, and totally deserted. He had never been without his family, not even for one day.

Joey slipped into the back seat next to Tootie. He leaned forward and gave Buddy's shoulder a playful nudge.

"Carls . . . catch!" Buddy said.

Joey nudged him again and then looked inquiringly at Tootie. "Is he visiting or st-staying?" he mouthed.

Tootie shook her head sadly. "Staying," she mouthed back. Quickly Tootie looked away. She kept staring at everything, memorizing the way to Fairbolt. She wanted to know every twist and turn and not miss a thing. "I want to be able to find Fairbolt on our own," Tootie confided quietly. "Help by watching where we go."

"Wh-what are you planning on doing?"

"I don't know," Tootie said shaking her head. "I honestly don't know!"

Father had obviously called ahead, because when they arrived at Fairbolt's large iron gate, Dr. Dunn was waiting for them with a huge smile. "Welcome," he greeted. His short, cropped, reddish hair looked more like peach fuzz than ever before. "You're on time," he announced. "That's a real rarity. I simply hate tardiness!"

Father drove the automobile slowly through the entrance, with the large branches of the crab apple tree hanging high above. Tootie heard the gate close firmly, and it set her nerves even more on edge. Father parked the car where Dr. Dunn directed, and they all got out. As always, Father wore his gray derby hat. But he had the narrow brim pulled down in the front and Tootie couldn't quite make out her father's expression.

Slowly they headed up the front steps past the white columns and the miniature potted trees. Finally they reached the carved front doors and Dr. Dunn pulled from his pocket a brass key about four inches long. With both hands, he unlocked the door and said with a flourish, "Welcome to your new home."

Chills ran over Tootie's entire body. She walked beside Buddy over the threshold into Fairbolt.

Father and Joey followed them into the lobby. It looked exactly the same as last Saturday—neat, clean, almost sterile. Dr. Dunn walked over to a shiny dark wood desk which was smack-dab in the middle of the room. A few comfortable-looking chairs were arranged squarely in front of the desk, just as in Dr. Dunn's downtown office. But besides that, there was not one other piece of furniture in the entire lobby: no comfortable sofa by the window or in front of the immaculately clean fireplace, not even a bookcase. There was absolutely no look of warmth or friendliness, and the white walls seemed to shout, *Don't linger! Get out of this place as fast as you can!*

Tootie knew her imagination must be going wild because when Dr. Dunn looked at her, his whole peachy appearance seemed genuine and concerned. "I can tell that you are leery of Fairbolt, young lady. Let me put your mind at ease." He opened the top drawer of the desk and pulled out a scrapbook. "Here, why don't you and your friend take a few minutes and look through these pages." The doctor looked at Tootie and then at Joey. "These pictures show some of our inmates at play. They also show some art work from our inmates, which I think you will enjoy. We encourage individualism at Fairbolt."

Tootie held the book to her chest. She glanced over at Buddy. He was still standing just inside the front door looking around the lobby with a hopeful expression saying, "Carls . . . catch!" every few minutes.

Grasping his billed cap in his right hand, Joey hit it several times against the palm of his left. "Wh-why do you call the people who live here inmates?" he blurted out. "It sounds like a p-prison, or something."

Dr. Dunn laughed. "Is that what's bothering you and Miss McCarthy? I was wondering. You both seem as rigid as patients I've observed with advanced cases of poliomyelitis." Then the doctor's small eyes narrowed. "By any chance, have you seen bars on the windows of this estate that I don't know about?"

"No," Joey answered.

Tootie reluctantly shook her head.

"Well," Dr. Dunn said and smiled in a tolerant, under-standing fashion, "let me try and explain about the word 'inmate.' It's simple. I read the term in a book and I liked the word. I don't mean anything negative by it. Not at all. This is no prison!" Then he paused. "Maybe it would sound better to you if I called all the residents at Fair-bolt, 'patients.' Would that suit you better?"

"No," Tootie said.

Her father looked uncomfortable. He turned his gray hat round and round in his hands. "Excuse my daughter and her friend. This is difficult for them. It's hard on all of us. In fact," he stopped and looked over toward Buddy, making sure he was far enough away so he couldn't hear. Then Father leaned slightly forward, put his hat up to the side of his face and quietly mouthed, "We haven't explained anything to Buddy. He believes he's coming for a visit to see that little fellow, Charles." Father shook his head sadly, "I didn't have the heart to tell him he's staying. Neither did my wife."

Just then Buddy walked over to the window and pulled back the heavy curtain. He dropped the little suitcase at his feet and took out the softball from his pants pocket.

Tootie noticed that the windows were clear; there were no bars in sight.

"I've never seen such pathetic expressions in all my life," the doctor admitted. "I'm sure Charles is busy this morning, but let me see what I can do. Maybe he can come and play catch with the boy."

They all watched as Dr. Dunn pushed a buzzer which was taped to the top of the desk. The wire from the small electric contraption ran down the leg of the desk and across the wide expanse to a door. Then the wire disappeared under the door and a buzzing sound could be heard coming from the opposite side. Tootie had no idea that the door was locked until she heard someone approach and unlock it. Miss Bonzer appeared in her starched uniform with her nurse's cap pinned to her tightly permed hair.

"Yes, Doctor," she said in her no-nonsense manner.

"The McCarthys have arrived, and they have brought our new inmate. I mean—they have brought Buddy. I believe it would do the entire family good to see the little fellow, Charles. You know, the youngster who played ball with Buddy last Saturday? I realize this is most unusual, but would you please go and bring the boy?"

"Certainly, Doctor," Nurse Bonzer responded. Her expression did not change one iota. The tightly-girdled nurse turned on her thick-soled shoes and went out the door through which she entered, locking it behind her.

Tootie couldn't imagine living in a place with locks

and keys. She walked over to the door, next to the one where Nurse Bonzer had just exited, and tried the doorknob. To her surprise, the door swung open. It was the same small room which the nurse had shown them on their first visit. It was the sample bedroom which was supposed to be like the one Buddy would get. It had a single bed with a red-and-blue checkered quilt and several fluffy pillows. The room even had a bureau with a mirror and a good-sized braided oval rug.

"It looks pleasant," Father said from behind her. He put his hands on her slender shoulders. "Our Buddy will enjoy a room like this, won't he, lass? He will be well taken care of here at Fairbolt. And this will give your mother a chance to get better."

"Oh, Father!" is all Tootie could say.

Joey hurried over to look out the window with Buddy.

Dr. Dunn stepped close to Donald and straightened the stethoscope which hung around his neck. "Our policy is that you do not visit right away. Let your son get used to the place, Mr. McCarthy. It's best that way. Less confusion."

"How long?" Donald asked.

Tootie interrupted. "I want to come back tomorrow to see him. What if he doesn't like it here?"

Dr. Dunn's stethoscope almost slid from around his neck as he jerked to attention. "Under no circumstances should you come tomorrow. That's entirely too soon for your brother. No, he will need at least one month to adjust."

"One month!" both Donald and Tootie gasped.

"Believe me," Dr. Dunn continued, "your son will do just fine here at Fairbolt. He'll adjust quickly. We have a lot of experience with these kinds of things. I will give him a thorough examination and he will also be given tests to see what he's capable of doing. Then we'll understand his potential. By the way, Mr. McCarthy, have you brought the payment we discussed?"

"Yes," Donald answered and brought out the three-thousand-dollar check from the inner pocket of his suit jacket.

Dr. Dunn took the check, turned, and walked out of the small bedroom into the lobby. He put it into the top drawer of the desk. Then he picked up the scrapbook that Tootie had laid on top of the desk and dropped it into the drawer, on top of the check. "Don't worry, Mr. McCarthy," the doctor said in an understanding manner. "Every parent feels the same when they first leave their child. It's a hard decision. But you are doing the very best for your boy and for your wife. You are a wise and brave man." He shut the desk drawer firmly and locked it. "I'll put that check into the bank first thing Monday morning. Meanwhile, it'll be safe here."

Father took out his handkerchief and wiped his brow.

Just then Charles came into the lobby from the front entrance with Nurse Bonzer. He looked at Buddy and smiled. "Come on," Charles said, "let's go outside and play catch!"

"Carls!" Buddy ran in his awkward way toward his new friend. He quickly handed the softball to Charles. They ran outside together.

"See," Dr. Dunn said, "Buddy is already feeling at home. You had better leave while he's playing ball. Don't worry." He held up his hands as he looked at their alarmed expressions. "I'll explain it all to him as best I can. Buddy will be just fine. Believe me. I'm used to this sort of thing."

"Listen to the doctor," Nurse Bonzer admonished. "We will take good care of your boy."

Why doesn't that sound reassuring? Tootie asked herself as she numbly scooted over next to her father in the front seat of the Model T. Joey cranked the engine and then slid in beside her.

But the moment they drove out of Fairbolt property and Tootie heard the big iron gate clang shut, she felt as if something deep inside her closed and locked forever. "Buddy!" she cried. "I can't leave my Buddy Boy!"

The rest of the day was awful. The McCarthy family walked around as if their world had come to an end. Donald sent Mrs. Roseen home, and the cleaning of the bakery was left unfinished.

That evening around the supper table, there was a minimum of talk. Instead, they all kept staring at Buddy's empty chair.

Even Pearl was miserable. "I miss him," she said gloomily. "I never dreamed I'd miss Buddy so much, especially at eating time. What do you think he's having for dinner?"

No one answered.

Tootie watched her father as he pushed the cooked cabbage around his plate. He searched through the limp, lukewarm pile until he found a small piece of ham. Finally he speared it with his fork, and the noise of his fork scraping across the plate sent chills up and down Tootie's arms. She had never seen her father so depressed.

"Donald, are you all right?" Mother asked from her makeshift bed on the sofa. She had been sick most of the day. A piece of dry toast and a cup of tea sat untouched on a small table next to her.

Father pushed his plate away, leaned back, and looked up at the ceiling. "I didn't think it would be this hard."

"Me, either," Pearl admitted and wiped her eyes with her napkin. "I even miss his messiness."

Mother's response was a deep, sad sigh. "It's all my fault. If I'd just get better!"

"None of that, Eve," Donald admonished. "You'll get well soon, and then we'll go to Fairbolt and bring home our son!"

Pearl interrupted, "Do you think Buddy's having potato soup? You know how much he loves it."

"We didn't even get to see the kitchen at Fairbolt," Tootie said. "We shouldn't have left him there!" Tootie stared at her family with a mixture of anger and frustration.

Later that night, instead of sleeping in the same bed with Pearl, Tootie decided to sleep in Buddy's bed. She didn't change the sheets. She remembered how pleased he had been that very morning because he had not wet the bed. It seemed like ages ago. Tootie ran her fingers over the cool sheets and with every stroke of her hand, she missed him more.

She knew she should pray. But the more she thought about everything, the more angry she became. She was mad not only at God and everyone else in her family, but at herself as well. *I shouldn't have left him. I shouldn't have left him at Fairbolt without telling him the truth. Why did I leave it all for Dr. Dunn to explain?*

Tears streamed down her cheeks and soaked into

Buddy's pillow. "I'm sorry, Buddy," she whispered into the pillow. "I'm so sorry!"

In the silence that followed, Tootie heard Mother in the bathroom, being sick.

Long minutes passed before Pearl whispered, "How can you sleep in Buddy's bed? It would give me the absolute creeps!"

"It makes me feel closer to him," Tootie answered. And then she whispered her greatest fear, "Pearl, I have this awful feeling about Fairbolt."

"Like what?"

Tootie struggled to put her thoughts into words. "Oh . . . I don't know exactly."

"Well, it's a beautiful place," Pearl replied. "And Dr. Dunn seems to be a good doctor. And Buddy will have friends his own age to play with."

"I know all that," Tootie whispered. "It's just this feeling I've got. It's weird, but I don't trust those people. Something's not right. What if Buddy's in danger?"

"Oh, don't say that! You're scaring me. I'm sure Buddy's not in any danger. You've always had such a wild imagination."

"I have not!"

"You have, too. But let me tell you something," Pearl's voice became barely more than a whisper. "I'd give anything right now to have Buddy here. I'd rather have Buddy back home with us than get my stupid teeth fixed!"

"Oh, Pearl! Really?"

"I mean it, Tootie. I know I complain a lot. And I

know I don't do as much to help Buddy as you do. But I just can't stand it that he's gone. I miss him so much!"

Waves of loneliness engulfed Tootie, and she began to experience real physical pain. She hurt so badly that all she could do was hug Buddy's pillow and moan.

They didn't say another word. They both became wrapped in their own misery. Finally Pearl turned over and Tootie heard her cry herself to sleep.

The next morning, everyone was surprised when Father decided to go to church. He never went on a regular Sunday, only on Christmas and Easter. He reached for his gray derby hat and said simply, "Thought I'd go this morning."

Eve smiled from the sofa. "I'm glad, Donald. I'll want to hear all about the sermon when you get back."

Tootie and Pearl walked alongside Father the four blocks down Washington Street to the Alliance Bible Church. The early Minnesota morning was crisp and cold. There wasn't a hint of wind or rain. It would have been perfect if Buddy and Mother were there. Tootie longed to hold Buddy's hand and walk to church as a complete family.

When they arrived, several people asked about Eve's health and where Buddy was. Father, Pearl, and Tootie did their best to avoid giving a straight answer concerning Buddy. But mostly people were pleased to see Father, and they greeted him kindly. Even Pastor Myers made a point of coming to shake hands and welcome him.

The Staddlers came in late and sat directly in front of them. Joey scooted in next to Tootie.

The congregation stood for the first song. Tootie didn't feel like singing. She shared the hymnal with Joey, but she didn't even attempt to join in. Her mind was constantly on Buddy and what was happening at Fairbolt. Joey's voice cracked several times, and, for once, Tootie didn't even tease. It was on the last verse that the words finally caught her attention: "Jesus, Jesus, how I trust him! How I've proved him o'er and o'er!"

Just then Joey leaned close to Tootie and said in a low tone, "We've done th-that, Tootie. We've p-proved him before. Remember the time when we had to come up with a p-plan to show Pearl she was being tricked by that boyfriend of hers?"

How could I forget that? Tootie thought.

"And remember how you n-needed an angel costume for the Christmas play? God worked it all out."

"But this is different!" In her frustration, Tootie didn't lower her voice.

"Shush!" Mrs. Staddler said over her shoulder. Then she continued singing with the congregation.

"We n-need to trust God this time, too," Joey continued. "We need to trust God that Fairbolt is the b-best place for Buddy."

"Joey Staddler, we don't have to do any such thing! God may want us to investigate the place!"

Just then Mrs. Staddler turned completely around and glared at them. She wore an enormous, ridiculous-looking hat. "Shush!" she said again. This time she said it so loud that the entire congregation heard. Even Father looked down the row and frowned.

After everyone sat down, Pastor Myers walked forward and stood behind the pulpit. He opened his huge black Bible and waited. He waited so long before beginning his sermon that Tootie finally glanced up from her clasped hands. To her total surprise, Pastor Myers was staring right at her.

Then he began, "The message today is from the Gospel of Matthew, chapter ten. I have always puzzled over verse sixteen, and during this past week I've given it much thought." Then he began to quote the verse. And Tootie was certain that while he was speaking his eyes never wandered from hers.

"Behold, I send you forth as sheep in the midst of wolves; be ye therefore wise as serpents, and harmless as doves."

It was as though a bolt of electricity shot through her. She sat ramrod-straight and listened to every word.

"Try to picture what Jesus is saying in this passage," Pastor Myers continued. "Imagine what it would be like for a sheep to be surrounded by a pack of wolves. Do you see the picture? Frightening, isn't it. Well, that's what Jesus said it would be like for the disciples. They would be like sheep among wolves. And that's exactly how it is with us."

Tootie grasped Joey's arm. "He's right," she whispered.

"Listen," Pastor Myers continued and he pointed around the audience, "the presence of wolves on every hand was a fact in Jesus' day, and it's a fact today. There are wolves out there who are dressed to look like sheep. You realize, of course, that Jesus was not talking literally about animals. Jesus was referring to people. In fact, this kind of person may be sitting here in the congregation this morning."

Tootie sucked in her breath. She glanced at Joey and then stole a look over her shoulder at the people crowded together in the pew behind.

"That's it!" Pastor Myers said. "Look around. Look into your neighbor's eyes. Wolves in sheep's clothing are hard to spot. They're devious, sly characters who appear to be good, moral, and often gentle. You can't spot them by looking, can you? So, my dear friends, beware!"

Tootie almost came right out of her pew.

Several people looked around, but most held their breath and waited for Pastor Myers to continue.

"Each and every one of us here this morning must show a combination of wisdom and courage in our dealings with wolves. How wise have you been this week? Have you been fooled by a wolf in a sheep's outfit? Scripture says that we are to be wise as serpents—that's another name for snakes you know—and as harmless as doves. What a contrast. Snakes and birds! Have you demonstrated discernment this week? Or have you been gullible? I beg of you, have a combination of wariness and innocence in all of your dealings. And by all means —whatever you do—pray! Pray daily. Pray hourly. Do not face wolves in sheep's clothing without prayer."

Pastor Myers went on and on, but Tootie took time out to think. *Could Dr. Dunn and Nurse Bonzer be wolves dressed up to look like innocent sheep?*

Joey must have been thinking the same thing because he whispered, "We've g-got to get Buddy out of F-Fairbolt!"

Mrs. Staddler turned around again and glared at them. But Tootie and Joey didn't even notice. They were trying to devise a plan—a plan where they could be as wise as serpents and as harmless as doves.

On the way out of church, Father shook Pastor Myers's hand. "Good advice you gave these people," Donald admitted. "I even learned a few things myself."

"Glad to hear it," Pastor Myers said with a smile. "None of us should ever stop learning. And sometimes we can even learn from the young." He reached out and patted Tootie on the shoulder. "Isn't that right, young lady?"

"That's right," Tootie said while ideas of how to rescue her brother flashed through her mind. *How can I be as sneaky as a snake and as harmless as a bird?* she wanted to ask. But she didn't dare. *Someone might try to stop me from rescuing my brother!*

Quickly she caught up with Joey.

"Wh-what's the plan?" Joey said as soon as he felt certain no one could hear.

Tootie looked around and noticed that Father and Pearl were starting for home. A cold wind blew past them and Father placed his derby hat at a jaunty angle and nodded at her. She nodded back, proud of the way her father looked. Then she whispered to Joey, "Can we use your bike? We can ride out to Fairbolt right after lunch."

"I guess," Joey said. "B-but what then? That g-gate's always locked!"

"I don't know *how* we'll get into the place, but I know we *will*. We have to, Joey. I'm sure Buddy's in danger. I feel it in my bones."

Just then Pearl came marching toward them. "For pity's sake, Tootie McCarthy, aren't you coming? I'm hungry, and we need to check on Mother. Do you expect us to wait forever?" Pearl's fake front teeth slipped up and down as she talked.

Tootie whispered quickly to Joey, "I'll meet you in back of your store in two hours."

Exactly two hours later, Tootie ran out of the apartment in an old pair of hand-me-down pants, her winter coat, and red scarf. She had told her parents that she needed some fresh air. The dishes were done, Mother was in bed after a bad bout of stomach cramps, and Father was reading *The Tribune*. Pearl had taken down the Sears catalog and was obviously daydreaming over the latest styles. Never for a minute had Tootie thought it would be this easy to get away.

Joey was waiting for her. He not only had *his* bike, but a second one which his father had repaired for another delivery boy. Both bikes had wire baskets attached to the front for carrying groceries. "Here, try this," Joey said as Tootie approached.

Tootie stared at the bike Joey offered and wondered how in the world her short legs were ever going to reach those pedals. She swung her leg over the seat. She realized that if she stood up as she pedaled, it could be done. "Before we go," Tootie said as she slid off the bike, "I . . . I want to ask God for help like Pastor Myers said."

"Sure," Joey responded as if praying together were something they did every day.

The two bowed their heads in the back alley. "Dear God," Tootie began as she clung to the grimy handlebars, "I'm sorry for the way I've been acting. I have been mad at everyone for letting this happen to Buddy. I haven't been trusting you like Mother told me to."

"I-I haven't either," Joey interrupted.

"But now we want to do what Pastor Myers talked about in the sermon."

"Th-that's right," Joey interrupted again. "We want to be s-sneaky like snakes and harmless as b-birds."

"Please help us." Tootie asked.

They both said, "Amen."

Tootie looked at Joey. "Let's go!"

Not another word was said as they rode their bikes down Washington Street. They both remembered the way exactly. Soon they had reached the outskirts of the city and were heading into the country toward the asylum. Tootie sat up on the seat of the bike to rest as she coasted down a hill. The cold wind stung her face.

Around the next bend in the road, she saw Fairbolt far ahead. It was set back among some trees, and from this distance it looked innocent and inviting. But somehow in her heart, she knew different.

She pedaled faster.

When they turned off the main road, they got off their bikes and walked them cautiously up to the gate. Joey tried the gate. It was locked.

"Over this way," Tootie whispered. She leaned her bike against the eight-foot fence as she wondered how they could be as innocent as birds. She looked up at large branches of the crab apple tree hanging over the fence. *Birds fly!* she reasoned. "Joey, if I climb onto this bike, I just might reach that branch. Hold the bike still."

Joey managed to balance the bike against the fence and make sure Tootie didn't fall. "C-can you reach it?"

Tootie didn't answer as she tried to keep her footing while standing on the seat of the bike and reaching for the lowest branch. She swung her legs up and climbed into the tree. Then she turned around and leaned down to help Joey. He looked determined, and soon he was sitting in the crab apple tree next to her.

"Good," Tootie said. Her voice sounded brave, but there was fear in her hazel eyes. She looked around quickly and then started scooting from branch to branch. Finally she and Joey reached the lowest branch inside Fairbolt property. "I guess this is the part where we begin to act like snakes."

"Guess s-so," Joey said. "I don't think Dr. Dunn or Nurse Bonzer would appreciate us s-snooping around."

Tootie was about to drop down out of the tree when Joey grabbed her arm. "Wait! You can't go in there w-wearing that!" He pointed to the red scarf. "They'll s-see you for sure!"

Tootie yanked off her scarf and threw it through the tree to the other side of the fence. Then she said, "Your black-and-white plaid jacket is just about as bad."

Joey took it off and flung it after Tootie's scarf. "I guess s-snakes don't wear plaids or red wool scarves," Joey said seriously.

A slight giggle escaped Tootie's trembling lips. She scanned the grounds and then cautiously lowered herself out of the tree.

Joey followed.

They lay flat in the grass and slowly moved forward. They spotted several small trees ahead, and then they both crouched low and ran. Hiding behind two of them, they peeked around. The place still looked quiet, almost as if no one were home. The curtains at every window were drawn tight. All of a sudden, drops of perspiration appeared on Tootie's face and chills ran up and down her spine. *Why would they keep the curtains closed unless they had something to hide? And why aren't children out here playing?*

Just then Tootie saw a curtain move on the second floor. She pulled back behind the tree.

Joey must have seen it too because his face looked white as he stammered, "S-someone's looking!"

Maybe it's Buddy, Tootie thought. Very carefully she peeked around the trunk of the tree and looked to the second floor. It wasn't Buddy at all. It was Nurse Bonzer. And to Tootie's horror, the nurse was looking through thick bars! She was leaning against the bars, glancing down the road as if she were expecting company.

"Bars!" Tootie mouthed over to Joey. Desperately she tried to hold back the panic which threatened to paralyze her. "Joey, there are *bars* on those windows!"

Anger rose in Tootie and almost choked out her fear. She glanced around the tree again and saw the curtains on the second floor were closed as tightly as the rest. Suddenly she darted out from behind the tree. She didn't even crouch low. She ran at full speed to the front of Fairbolt and hid behind one of the huge white columns.

Joey followed more cautiously and finally stumbled up the front stairs. "What are you t-trying to prove?" he said. "Getting c-caught isn't going to help!"

Tootie knew Joey was right. Quietly she tiptoed around the column and headed straight to the front door and slowly turned the knob. The huge carved double doors were locked. "Let's go around to the back," she whispered over her shoulder. "There must be another way into this place."

"There is," whispered Joey. "When I was p-pretending to play with Buddy and that Charles boy, I s-saw the back entrance. Th-this way."

Joey led Tootie around the side of the building. They stayed as low as they could. As they approached the back entrance, they heard talking coming from inside the house.

All of a sudden Tootie's bravery vanished and her entire body became stiff, as if she were frozen in place. She couldn't make herself move.

Joey grabbed her arm and pulled her behind a long row of garbage cans. Just as they fell to the ground, the back door opened and they heard several people come out. Neither Tootie nor Joey dared look. They could hardly breathe. Not just the stench from the garbage made their stomachs reel, but their absolute terror as well. Joey was still holding on to her, and she could feel his whole body quivering.

When he began to talk they immediately recognized the voice of Dr. Dunn. "Slow up, man! I've been looking all over the place for you."

"What's so almighty important that you have to follow me out here?" The second man's words were sharp.

"I want to use your son Charles again today. We have some parents coming with their half-wit boy. I think they're moneyed people, and I'm hoping they've brought the amount I told them."

The other man chuckled wickedly. "You fool more people!"

Dr. Dunn's voice sounded pleased as he said, "I've got to get several checks into the bank first thing tomorrow morning. Anyway, that's no concern of yours."

Tootie heard the other man swear.

"All I want you to do," Dr. Dunn continued, "is have your boy come into the lobby and offer to play with their stupid child. You know, like Charles did yesterday when we admitted that McCarthy boy."

"I remember," answered Charles's father. Then he must have held out his hand because Tootie heard Dr. Dunn slap a bill across his palm.

"Don't get greedy," Dr. Dunn said. "That's all you're getting. Nurse Bonzer will ring the buzzer from the lobby sometime after four this afternoon. That will be your signal to have Charles ready and send him in. Understand?"

The other man must have nodded.

Then Dr. Dunn laughed. "Your boy is so convincing! Puts parents right at ease. They probably think he's a cured half-wit!"

Tootie and Joey heard Charles's father curse as he turned away from Dr. Dunn and walked toward the garbage cans. He threw a few sacks onto the heap and stormed back into the house after the doctor, slamming the door behind him.

Tootie and Joey stared at each other. They were both shaking so violently that for a while they couldn't speak. Finally Tootie swallowed hard and whispered, "Do you think anyone will ever believe this?"

"Th-they've got to!"

Then one of the sacks, which had been haphazardly thrown onto the garbage, fell off. The contents spilled all over Tootie and Joey. And in the midst of the mess were Buddy's blue pajamas. They were the ones that Tootie had packed for him. She knew for certain they were Buddy's by the small holes which he had worn in the material with his constant rubbing.

"Look!" Tootie cried. She reached out and grabbed the blue pajamas. They were damp and Tootie knew Buddy must have wet his bed. "Why would they throw away Buddy's pajamas?" She didn't even think about keeping her voice low.

The sight of Buddy's pajamas worked like a shot of adrenaline to Joey. He grabbed Tootie's arm so hard that it hurt. "Th-this is just what we need. These pajamas will p-prove something's wrong. Let's get out of here!"

Tootie didn't want to leave. She wanted to storm into Fairbolt and demand the release of her brother.

Joey stared for a moment at Tootie's determined expression. Then he said, "All we have to do is sh-show these pajamas to the authorities. They'll know what to do."

Tootie nodded, her face reflecting her struggle. In her heart she knew Joey was right.

They darted out from behind the garbage cans. But as they ran, Tootie felt certain someone was watching. She was desperately hoping it was God and not Nurse Bonzer from the upstairs window.

Tootie arrived at the crab apple tree first. She shinned up the trunk until she reached a branch and then clung to it with all her strength. For a second, she had a flashback of the Gypsy boy, Leon, shinning up the light pole outside of Logan School the night they were searching for Pearl. Somehow it brought an unexpected spurt of energy. *Leon made it—and so will we!* With great effort, Tootie swung herself up onto the branch.

Turning around quickly, she saw Joey, pulling himself up after her. For a second they stared at each other with wide, frightened eyes. Then they scooted carefully from branch to branch. Finally Tootie moved out onto the branch that hung over the high fence. She jumped and knocked over the bikes.

"Buddy's pajamas!" she whispered hoarsely and grabbed her skinned knee. "We forgot them!" She bit her trembling lower lip and looked up at Joey who was still in the tree, ready to jump.

Joey stretched his suspenders and pulled the wet evidence from inside his shirt. He let the pajamas drop to the ground.

Tootie grabbed them and the bikes, moving everything out of Joey's way. He jumped.

Tootie frantically stuffed Buddy's pajamas, along with her red scarf, into the wire basket and took off, following Joey.

The race into town seemed to go on for ever. Tootie kept wishing with all her heart that Buddy were escaping with them. She felt guilty that she had left him behind at that awful place.

They raced on with their shoulders bent low against the cold, late afternoon breeze. Joey hadn't taken time to put on his plaid coat and his shirt billowed out around his suspenders as he sped along.

Tears of fright and frustration began streaming down Tootie's pale cheeks as they turned onto Washington Street. They were about to pass the Alliance Bible Church when Pastor Myers came down the stairs, whistling. "Good evening," he greeted.

Tootie and Joey were so intent on getting home and telling the news that they sped right past him.

"Wait!" Pastor Myers shouted. "Hold it!"

Joey skidded to a stop and Tootie almost plowed into the back of his bike. Pastor Myers hurried over. "What's going on? What's wrong?"

Tootie gasped, trying her best to answer. "They're holding Buddy prisoner at the asylum! We've got to hurry!"

"Slow up," their pastor insisted. "Start from the beginning. Are you talking about Fairbolt?"

"Th-that's right," Joey said. "Th-there are bars on the windows, and th-they've taken Buddy's pajamas. Here's p-proof!" and he pointed to Tootie's scarf, which was covering Buddy's blue pajamas.

"What in the world?" Pastor Myers looked puzzled. "You two aren't making any sense, and you're both scared half out of your minds."

Tootie grabbed her scarf and then held up Buddy's pajamas. "These are my brother's," she shouted. "Those people back there are holding my brother prisoner!"

"Where in the world did you find those?"

"At Fairbolt!" Tootie and Joey said at the same time.

"I don't trust that place!" Pastor Myers said. "There's an uneasiness right here whenever Fairbolt is mentioned." Their pastor hit his muscular chest.

"Come with us!" Tootie shouted as she and Joey hurried back to their bikes.

Pastor Myers fairly ran down Washington Street after Tootie and Joey all the way to the McCarthys. He arrived shortly after them, took a moment to hide the bikes behind the apartment steps out of sight of passersby, and hurried into the McCarthy's apartment after Tootie and Joey.

Mother was lying on the couch, Father was sitting at the table working on their financial books, and Pearl was still dreaming over pictures in the Sears catalog when they burst into the room.

Tootie and Joey began blurting out the events of the past few hours.

Father, Mother, Pearl, nor Pastor Myers said a word. They all sat completely still, almost dumfounded. They kept staring at Tootie and Joey as if every word that was being said were absolutely unbelievable.

Finally the pencil in Father's hand snapped. "Did you say you saw bars? Are you positive, lass?"

"Yes, Father—bars! Nurse Bonzer was looking through them."

"Now let me get this straight." Donald stood up and began pacing the floor, fidgeting all the while with the lapels of his suit.

"Why—why that means that Dr. Dunn is an out-and-out liar!"

Pastor Myers interrupted, "But any asylum would have bars. I'm sure that's regulation."

Donald frowned. "Then why would that doctor lie about it? He definitely told us there were no bars at Fairbolt. He made a point of it. We don't want our little lad behind bars!"

"What do you think is going on?" Mother asked and rubbed her stomach. Her whole expression was pained.

Tootie held up Buddy's pajamas. "Look!" she said.

"Those are Buddy's!" Mother cried. "How did you get them?"

Joey stepped forward. "They were th-thrown into the garbage can, Mrs. McCarthy. You sh-should have heard the way Dr. Dunn talked. And remember that Charles boy? Well, he's in on this whole sc-scheme!"

Tootie went on to dramatize the whole scene she and Joey had overheard while hiding behind the garbage bins at the asylum.

Once again everyone listened intently, but this time Pastor Myers began pacing along with Father. They both shook their heads with great agitation.

Pearl reached out and stuck her finger through one of the holes in Buddy's pajamas. The moment she did it, she broke into loud crying.

Mother was also crying. "You don't think they'll hurt our laddy boy, do you?"

"No," Donald answered quickly. "I don't think they'd harm him. I just think they're out for money." Donald hit the top of the old Miester piano. "What a fool I've been! I should never have trusted those people without looking into it."

"I'll call the authorities," Pastor Myers suggested.

Mother's condition worsened and she hurried into the bathroom.

It wasn't long before two police officers arrived at the McCarthys. One of them was Officer Riley who worked the Washington Street area.

"Don't worry," Officer Riley responded when he had heard the story. He was very fat and his shirt stretched open between each button. "We'll get the proper papers first thing tomorrow morning, and we'll go right out there and investigate."

"Tomorrow!" Tootie yelled. "What do you mean, tomorrow? Buddy needs to get out of there tonight!"

"Not so fast, young lady," Officer Riley said. "It's not

that easy. Especially on Sunday—being short of staff and all."

Father continued pacing. Eve had just returned to the room, and he went over and put his arm around her.

"Do you think our son is in any danger?" Eve asked.

"No," the officer said. "It sounds to me like those people are simply out for the big bucks. I don't believe anyone is in danger—except for the danger of losing your money."

Father moaned.

"There must be something we can do!" Pastor Myers said.

"Now, now, everyone. You realize that these things take time." The other officer spoke for the first time. He didn't wear a name tag and Tootie had missed his name when he introduced himself.

"Are you going to expose this place as a fraud?" Donald asked.

"Maybe . . . maybe not," Officer Riley said, as if he had been deep in contemplation. "Let's first find out the facts. Like I said, we need to have the right papers with us when we go. If we rush too quickly into these things, we may hurt the situation—if you know what I mean."

Pastor Myers interrupted. "Have you had any complaints about Fairbolt before?"

"No," the officer without the name tag answered. "At least, not as far as we know. We'll look into that too." He had a pleasant look and appeared to be in his late twenties. "This whole situation may be a complete misunderstanding. The establishment may be on the up-and-up. And I agree with the pastor here—there's nothing strange about bars on an asylum. Who wants crazy people escaping and running around town?"

Every one of the McCarthys stiffened. Father said sternly, "Our boy's not crazy! He's only in that place to give my wife some needed rest. This whole thing was Dr. Dunn's idea. And it was only going to be for a short time . . . just until Eve regained her strength."

"Is that the reason?" Pastor Myers asked. "I wondered why Buddy had been admitted, but I didn't feel free to ask. If that's the case, I'm sure our church people can help."

"Really?" Eve said hopefully.

"Nothing doing!" Father said. "We McCarthys are proud people. We don't take handouts from anybody. We pay our way."

Pastor Myers blinked and then said with a steady voice, "This isn't a handout, Donald. It's God's people helping one another. I'm sure someone from our congregation would love to volunteer a helping hand until Eve gets better."

Tootie thought it sounded wonderful.

"No," Father said again. "We'll get our lad home and somehow we'll manage."

"Whatever," Officer Riley said impatiently. "Now, let's get back to the issue at hand."

Pastor Myers shifted his weight. "This whole Fairbolt situation is preposterous!"

"That it is," Father added.

"What about Buddy's pajamas?" Pearl cried. "Why would they throw them away?" She reached out to hold Tootie's hand.

"Who knows?" Officer Riley answered. "They may have regulation pajamas at that place. Oh, by the way, if Fairbolt isn't on the level—you know, legitimate—I think there'll be something of a reward. I know the Governor is real careful about this sort of thing. Clamping down hard, so to speak."

"Let's not talk about any reward," Mother said through her tears. "I just want my son to be happy and safe! I miss him so much!" Eve sat down on the sofa and almost doubled over in pain.

"Are you all right, lady?" Officer Riley asked.

"Like I said, my wife's been ill," Donald explained as he patted Eve on the shoulder.

"Well, rest assured," Officer Riley said as he proudly puffed out his chest and flabby belly. "We'll turn that place upside down tomorrow morning and make sure everything's legit. And if there's anything dishonest going on out there—we'll know it. Meanwhile, your son's fine for tonight. Trust me!"

Tootie wished with all her heart that she could feel reassured. But she didn't. There was a horrible feeling of doom crowding in around her and pressing her down, down, down almost to the point of despair.

A fter the police officers left, Pastor Myers asked to talk privately with Tootie and Joey before he went back to the church. They walked him outside and they stood on the steps together.

"What prompted you to go out to Fairbolt?" Pastor Myers asked them.

"It was because of your sermon," Tootie said in surprise. "You told us to be sneaky like snakes and as harmless as doves. So we thought you meant for us to go out to Fairbolt and investigate."

"Th-that's right," Joey added. "We th-thought you were giving us some sort of instructions. And then when you talked about wolves in sh-sheep's clothing, w-we thought you meant Dr. Dunn and Nurse Bonzer."

Pastor Myers leaned against the railing. "Hmmmm, I never intended. . . . But it just might be that the Holy Spirit was doing His work. Now, mind you, God never wants us to break the law by sneaking into places. That's not right. But God may very well have wanted

Fairbolt investigated. In fact, I'd say that's obvious. Hmmmm . . . ."

Tootie and Joey looked at each other.

"I do appreciate the way you two try to apply God's Word, put it into practice, so to speak," the pastor continued. "You don't just want to be hearers; you're doers. Isn't that right?"

"Ahhh . . . I guess so, sir," Tootie answered.

Joey nodded.

"There are many incidences in the Bible where God turned bad situations around completely. He is able to make the most horrible situation turn out for good."

Tootie had a hard time believing any good could come from Buddy being in an asylum, but she desperately hoped Pastor Myers was right.

"Before I leave, I want to have a word of prayer about this whole situation." Pastor Myers immediately began to pray for Buddy's protection during the night, his quick release from Fairbolt, and for the McCarthy's financial problems.

Tootie had never heard such a simple but sincere prayer. In a way, it reminded her of listening and watching Buddy when he communed with the Almighty. *Both Buddy and Pastor have the same kind of trust*, Tootie thought with genuine longing.

After Joey and Pastor Myers left, the rest of the evening dragged on. There was a lot of crying, and consoling, and discussion of the right or wrong of Tootie and Joey sneaking into Fairbolt. Tootie didn't know how much more she could take.

"I'm going to bed," she finally announced.

"Good," Father said. "In fact, we all should have an early bedtime. We want to be ready to leave first thing in the morning."

After Tootie and Pearl were in bed, they could hear their parents talking quietly in the other bedroom. Every once in a while they heard Eve running to the bathroom and being sick.

Pearl's voice came from across the room to Buddy's bed where Tootie was lying. "Are you still awake?"

"Yes."

"Let me tell you something, Tootie" Pearl said. "Right now, all I care about is Buddy. He's more important than anything. And I don't care about us getting any reward. I just want my brother back home! Maybe we *should* quit school so we can help."

Tootie couldn't believe the change in Pearl.

Pearl sighed and then continued, "That was a brave thing you did today . . . going out to Fairbolt and all."

"Thanks."

"I couldn't have done it for the world!" Pearl paused for a long time. Finally she continued, "I heard Mother scolding you, but I still think it was brave. Even if Father does get our money back from that Dr. Dunn, I don't want it used for my teeth. I think we should pay someone to watch Buddy and to help with Mama. That way maybe we won't have to quit school." Then she paused again as if she had finished.

Tootie turned over and faced the wall.

"Poor Buddy!" Pearl said after several minutes had passed. "What's happening to him in there behind those awful bars and locked doors? Oh, Tootie, do you think he's all right? Do you think they've given him Fairbolt pajamas, or do you think they're making him sleep naked?"

Tootie didn't answer. That thought sent new chills down her spine. *They wouldn't!*

Pearl sighed again, turned over onto her stomach, and eventually went to sleep.

But Tootie couldn't. She tossed and turned. "Oh, God," she whispered into the still night air, "what should I do?"

Immediately she sat straight up. It was as if God popped the answer right into her brain. She knew exactly what needed to be done.

Quietly she pulled an old sweater over her head and then reached for the hand-me-down trousers she'd thrown onto the floor. She pulled them on and stuffed the long length of her nightgown inside. After grabbing her shoes, coat, and scarf, she crept to the bedroom door. Within minutes, she was out of the apartment and easing down the outside steps. She barely took time to slip on her shoes. The moon was bright and it lighted her way. The bikes were nowhere in sight. They weren't even behind the apartment steps where Pastor Myers had left them.

She glanced across Washington Street toward the Staddler Grocery Store. The lights in the store were

out, but the whole area was aglow because of Mr. Staddler's huge flood lights. She could see the big old vine-
gar keg in front of the store, and the worn boards of the
boardwalk.

Tootie hurried across the street and behind the store
to see if the bikes were there. Just as she arrived, Joey
came out of the back door wearing his plaid coat. "I th-
thought you'd come. I've been waiting."

They looked into each others eyes and they both knew
exactly what had to be done.

"But this time we won't go breaking into the place,"
Tootie whispered. "We'll go right up to the gate and
holler, if we have to. No sneaking over any fence. We'll
demand Buddy's release. I just know it's the right thing
to do. Hurry, I have this feeling there's no time to waste!"

The gas lamps down Washington Street cast eerie
shadows in the cold evening. Tootie and Joey stayed to
the side of the road as they pedaled furiously. There was
a sprinkling of people on the street, but mostly the town
was quiet.

Soon they were out in the country. The moon shone
brightly, and Tootie hollered, "See—God's lighting our
way!"

Joey didn't answer. He was riding beside her, and
every once in a while he glanced at her as though he
thought they were both half crazed.

Maybe we are crazy, Tootie thought. Suddenly an
unexplainable peace settled over her. It was as if God
were helping her pedal every inch of the way toward the
asylum.

"Joey," she yelled as they bounced over the gravelly road, "I think God's going to open the gate for us at Fairbolt."

"What makes you th-think that?"

"Because God wants us to rescue Buddy and he doesn't want us to break any laws. So I figure he must be going to open the gate for us." She leaned low and strained up the last remaining hill which stood between her and Fairbolt.

The moment they crossed the crest of the hill, they saw lights on in the asylum and a car parked in front. And, to Joey's surprise, the gate was wide open and so was the front door.

"See," Tootie whispered as they came to a dead stop. "Look!"

Joey didn't say a word.

They quickly parked their bikes against a tree and walked directly onto Fairbolt property. Tootie was leading the way, and she reached the front steps slightly before Joey.

Joey pulled her behind one of the pillars. His breathing was short and raspy.

"Be c-careful!"

Tootie peeked around the curve of the pillar. Finally she tiptoed up the steps and over to the door. She could hear voices and one of them was definitely Dr. Dunn.

"We've been waiting for you for hours," he said to the family, who were standing with him in the lobby. "We expected you around four this afternoon. It's now almost nine! What happened to delay you so long? I hate tardiness!"

"Sorry, Dr. Dunn," the father apologized. "We had car problems. It was the oddest thing. Our car just stalled for no apparent reason. We've been stranded for hours out in the countryside. And then, just a few minutes ago, it started up just as easy as could be."

"We've brought our boy, as you suggested," the mother added pitifully.

"And the payment," the father said.

"Well . . . in that case," Dr. Dunn said in a more cheerful tone, "let me ring this buzzer and ask Nurse Bonzer to come and assist. You are definitely doing the right thing. Your son will receive excellent care here at Fairbolt and his mental condition will begin improving. I promise!"

Tootie tiptoed back to Joey. She told him what she had heard, and then they both sneaked over to the window. The heavy curtains were open a few inches, and they watched as Nurse Bonzer came into the room. She didn't bring Charles with her, as they knew she had planned. *Maybe it's too late*, Tootie thought. Her heart was pounding so loudly that she thought for certain everyone within a mile could hear its beat.

Tootie and Joey continued watching as the sad parents, their retarded boy, Dr. Dunn, and Nurse Bonzer went into the small bedroom directly off the lobby.

"They're p-probably giving them the same story th-they gave your family," Joey stammered.

Tootie nodded with great disgust. Then she darted

away from the window. Before he could stop her, she had slipped into Fairbolt and was heading straight across the lobby toward the door with the buzzer. Nurse Bonzer hadn't relocked the door, and it opened easily as Tootie turned the knob.

For a moment, Joey stood deathly still. Then he, too, stole across the lobby and quickly entered the forbidden hallway. Silently, he closed the door behind them. They found themselves in a narrow, dim hall with a door at the other end. And to their horror, that door was bolted tight with a two-by-four plank resting in the latch across the full width.

Joey's eyes almost bulged out of their sockets.

Tootie's legs went weak. She seemed to be walking in slow motion as she stumbled down the passageway and almost fell against the bolted door.

Joey was immediately behind her, "We c-can't s-stay in this hallway! We'll be c-caught for s-sure!" Without another stutter, he lifted the two-by-four and very cautiously opened the door.

Tootie peeked in first; Joey followed. What they saw made them so angry that being afraid was suddenly the last thing on their minds.

"Bend over, Number 33," Charles's father bellowed to a quivering child, who was standing on the opposite side of the large room from Tootie and Joey.

The ward was filled with at least sixty pathetic inmates of all different ages. Some were listlessly stumbling about, but most huddled close to the cement walls or pressed their bodies against the iron bars which crisscrossed each window. Some were even hiding under blankets on the bare floor.

With increasing shock, Tootie noticed that each inmate's head had been shaved completely bald. All of them wore identical gray pajamas with numbers taped to their backs right between their shoulder blades. She scanned the room as best she could, but she couldn't spot Buddy anywhere.

"You're a dirty, wicked boy to do your leave-taking in your pants." Charles's father continued to bellow. "Bend over and grab your toes!" He cursed violently. "You're in for the whipping of your life!"

Tootie wanted to run over and rescue the little fellow.

Just then Joey yanked her coat sleeve and pointed to a curtained area directly to the right of the door. After quietly shutting the hallway door, they ran over and hid behind the curtain. They could hear the boy being beaten, and Tootie plugged her ears to try and keep out his pathetic cries.

"Wh-what kind of place is th-this?" Joey whispered. His face was ashen and tears brimmed in his frightened eyes.

"We've got to find Buddy!" Tootie whispered.

Joey motioned for her to keep her voice down. Frantically he looked around the small enclosure in which they were standing. It contained a cot, a chair, a locked glass cupboard with a few surgical instruments, and row upon row of drawers with labels taped to each. A pile of gray institutional pajamas filled in the corner next to a stack of blankets.

Tootie noticed the pajamas at the same time as Joey, and then they stared at each other. They both knew what they had to do. Quickly Joey took off his hat, and Tootie her scarf. Then they removed their coats and as much of their clothing as they could. Tootie had forgotten she'd left on her nightgown, but she was thankful. With trembling fingers she managed to pull on the regulation pajamas and stuff her nightgown down inside. Just being in the Fairbolt uniform, feeling the coarse material against her skin, and smelling the sour odor, set her nerves more on edge and made her stomach reel. Finally they removed their shoes and hid everything under the pile of blankets. After grabbing a blanket and covering their heads, they went back to the curtain and peeked out.

Charles's father had finished the beating, and they watched the youngster crawl away, whimpering. "If anyone else needs to do some leave-taking, use the lavatory!" he shouted. "Now, somebody's got to strip this boy and hose him down!" The man stormed back and forth and finally demanded, "All right, everybody, into the middle of the room." He motioned violently with his hands to show exactly what he wanted everyone to do. "Quit cowering against the windows and walls. And you two over there by the curtain—you know better than that! How can one man be expected to watch a room full of half-wits?"

Everyone started moving immediately toward the center of the floor. Tootie and Joey followed, all the while trembling under their blankets.

Just then Nurse Bonzer entered, pushing the new boy in front of her. Her ugly face was etched with tension. "Has anyone come into this room through this door?" she shouted to Charles's father.

"No! I've been looking after this entire lot all by myself. No one's come in—no one's left—through that door, nor this one. What's your problem?"

Nurse Bonzer visibly relaxed. "I was certain I bolted this hallway door when I went out to the lobby." She pointed to the door in which Tootie and Joey had entered. "I've never forgotten that before!"

The man laughed wickedly and then an arrogant

smirk spread across his face. "Just wait till the great and mighty Dr. Dunn hears you forgot once."

"Watch your mouth, Herman!" Nurse Bonzer hissed and her white-knuckled hands shook.

The man stood still, his eyes darting to and fro. Sweat ran down his furrowed forehead. Finally he swore an oath which made Tootie cringe. Then he marched across the ward, knocking several patients aside. Tootie stepped back, held her breath, and pulled the blanket further over her face as he stormed past her and Joey. Herman didn't even look their way. He reached out and grabbed the trembling new admission, who was standing in front of Nurse Bonzer.

The young boy was visibly upset as Herman began yanking off his clothes. He tried to protest by locking his thumbs in his trouser pockets. This so infuriated Charles's father that he slapped the youngster across the face. The moment the boy cowered, Herman finished stripping him until he stood naked in the middle of the room.

"You must obey everything I say," Herman shouted. "Obey in action and in spirit! If you don't, it'll be the wet-pack for you."

"Or electroshock therapy!" Nurse Bonzer added as she began pawing through the boy's clothes.

The entire crowd of inmates moved back. It was obvious they all knew exactly what the threats meant.

Then Nurse Bonzer picked up the new inmate's clothes, shoes, and small suitcase and went to the curtain, pushing it back. She flopped the case onto the cot and proceeded to take out all his personal belongings, fingering everything. Then she stuffed all his things into one of the drawers and marked a small white label attached to the front with his name: Robert Jones. "There," she said with satisfaction. "When those parents of yours come for a visit, we'll dress you up *real* fine. They'll never know what you wear everyday."

Herman laughed, and Tootie noticed that his arrogant smirk had returned. He proceeded to dress the confused boy in a pair of the foul-smelling pajamas. "Come on, make it snappy," he barked. "Don't make me do to you what I had to do yesterday with that new admission!" Herman laughed wickedly. "He was a stubborn one!"

Tootie gasped. She peeked sideways at Joey, who was trying his hardest to stay hidden under the blanket. She could hear his breathing coming in short angry huffs. Their eyes locked in horror as they realized the man must be talking about Buddy!

"From now on," Nurse Bonzer announced to the frightened new admission, "you're Number 64." She pressed a piece of tape with a bold 64 printed on it to the back of his pajamas. "Don't forget your number. You're no longer, Robert Jones. You're Number 64!"

"And you're a wicked boy, Number 64, because your folks kept us waiting." Herman spoke in a slow, threatening tone. "We expected you hours ago. None of us have eaten our supper. I only had time to put on the porridge for this crazy lot, and then I had to come in here—"

"Oh, shut up!" Nurse Bonzer snapped. "None of us care what you had to do."

Herman's scowling face turned dark. Tootie thought for certain he was going to hit the nurse.

Just then Dr. Dunn came into the ward. "What's going on? Why haven't you shaved his head? What's taking you so long to admit this boy?"

Herman turned his scowl towards the doctor. "Do I have to do *everything* around here?"

"If you want to keep this job, you do!" Dr. Dunn responded, and his face turned as red as his hair. Then he stuck out his barrel-shaped chest, "Forget the shaving. You can do it later. Get this group of lunatics into the dining room and feed them!"

Herman turned on his heels, stormed across the room, unlocked the door, and shouted, "Move it!"

To Tootie's and Joey's surprise, the entire group immediately crouched down and began jumping forward, frog fashion. Tootie and Joey crouched low and hopped with the others. It was hard to do with the blankets covering their heads, but they managed. They were herded down a narrow, dimly lit hallway and prodded into the most foul-smelling room Tootie had ever experienced. The smell hit her like a wave of sewer water. Tootie could see several bathtubs with slimy water on top and wet towels everywhere. Charles was leaning over one of the tubs, and he shouted to his father, "This water won't go down! Sink's clogged again!"

Herman swore. On his way to his son, he shouted to the boy he had previously whipped for messing his pants. He gave instructions to Charles to hose him down. Finally Herman turned to the cowering inmates, "Do your leave-taking! Last chance tonight!"

There were rows of greasy basins and filthy, cracked toilets. No doors anywhere for any privacy. Tootie pulled the blanket over her face so she wouldn't have to see.

Finally Herman herded the whole group into another ward. The inmates frog-hopped over to a long table where bowls were lined up. One by one they took a bowl and scampered off to a corner or along the wall of the ward to eat.

Tootie and Joey hopped over to the table and very quickly took a bowl. They hurried to a corner and huddled together, under their blankets. They each held a pewter bowl of porridge. They stared at the cereal and shivered. It contained lumps, hairs, and unexplainable black bits. The bowl had an overhanging rim and under the rim were layers of sour porridge. Tootie began flaking them off in long strips. "This is what they've given Buddy," she said in a strained voice. "Oh, Joey, what are we going to do?"

"I . . . I . . . I never dreamed any p-place could be this bad."

There was a loud commotion, and Tootie and Joey peeked out. They couldn't tell, at first, what was happening. Then they saw the new admission, Number 64, being shoved violently against the table.

"You idiot!" Dr. Dunn shouted at the confused and frightened child. "No one bites me and gets away with it!" He hit the boy several times across the face. "We pull the teeth from biters!"

"Or we administer electroshock therapy!" Nurse Bonzer interrupted. Her large, firm frame almost trembled with anticipation.

Tootie and Joey noticed that, once again, everyone in the room had a violent reaction to the words: *electroshock therapy*. Tootie wondered again what that could possibly mean.

"Good idea!" Dr. Dunn agreed. "We can't allow the inmates to think they can get away with biting the staff." Then he smiled and his small eyes were lost and hidden under his full, fuzzy eyebrows.

Nurse Bonzer smiled with satisfaction. "And remember we still have to teach that new inmate from yesterday that he can't steal his own pajamas and get away with it. That stupid boy wet his pajamas last night after he'd gone through all that trouble!"

Herman laughed along with Nurse Bonzer. "I threw them into the garbage earlier this afternoon when I was emptying the trash. Number 63 is quite a handful. I think we ought to use both him and Number 64 as examples."

Tootie thought it was obvious that Dr. Dunn didn't like taking suggestions from Herman. "I'll decide when electroshock therapy is necessary," he announced. "Number 63 has been put in a wet-pack, hasn't he?"

"Yes," Nurse Bonzer responded. "He's tied up good and tight."

"That'll do for tonight," Dr. Dunn said.

"But," Nurse Bonzer continued, "that boy didn't cry out like the others. Instead, he closed his eyes and began muttering something. It—it sounded suspiciously like he was praying."

"Praying!" Dr. Dunn gasped. "We can't have any of that! I've seen what happens when people pray." The doctor shivered as if he were recalling a particular incident, and his complexion matched his red hair. "Prayer can completely foil our plans."

Then Nurse Bonzer added, "And Number 63 also kept saying, 'Toot—Toot—Toot'. Can't figure it out."

Tootie couldn't stand any more. *What have they done to my Buddy Boy? What's a wet-pack? Where have they tied him?*

Joey grabbed her arm as she was about to fling back her cover, "D-don't," he warned. "If you let them s-see you, w-we'll never find Buddy."

"Oh, God," Tootie whispered in her anguish, "help us!"

A ll right," Herman bellowed as the inmates finished eating the dreadful porridge, "drop your bowls into the container on your way out. Get to your rooms. *Move it!*"

Tootie and Joey didn't know what to do. They hadn't eaten a bit of their porridge. And they knew that if they dropped their bowls full of the stuff into the container, they'd be discovered.

"W-we've g-got to eat it," Joey said.

Tootie didn't argue. She held her nose and tipped the bowl.

Joey did the same.

The inmates were hurrying to the door. Tootie and Joey nervously joined them. Herman was standing by a large tub, intently eyeing each person. Tootie and Joey were coming nearer and nearer to the front of the line. The closer they got, the more panicky they became. Herman yanked a blanket away from one of the inmates, and then began glaring at Tootie and Joey.

Just as he was about to grab their blankets, the inmate

in front of them dropped her bowl into the tub. A glob of porridge plopped out and landed on Herman's hand. His ugly face turned dark as he stared at the lumpy glob and then at the shaking inmate.

"Food's not good enough for you, huh? Think you're a grand duchess or something?" He grabbed the poor girl by the back of her neck and pulled her out of the line.

"Get to your rooms—all of you!" Nurse Bonzer demanded.

Everyone quickly finished filing out of the dining room and into a long corridor with numerous small bedrooms leading off both sides. Tootie and Joey didn't know where to go. The area was almost dark. Besides, they were finding it hard to maneuver under their blankets. In their panic, they stumbled into a narrow table which stood right in the middle of the corridor. The table had straps on both sides and wires at the head, which were attached to a strange-looking box with dials.

As the rest of the inmates passed, they steered clear of the table and nervously stepped back.

Tootie and Joey began frantically peering into each of the little rooms. "Buddy . . . Buddy," they called as quietly as possible.

Just then they heard Dr. Dunn yell a command from the dining room: "Put the new admission down in the last room on the left with Number 63. And, Nurse Bonzer, I want him put into a wet-pack."

Tootie's heart pounded. She felt certain Number 63 was Buddy. "That's Buddy's room!" she whispered to Joey.

They began walking with giant strides down the long

hallway to the last room on the left. To their surprise, the door was wide open. A boy was wrapped in a dirty jacket and strapped tightly to the bed. The mattress had been removed; it was leaning against the far wall. The victim was lying on the bare wooden slats of the bed, facing away from the door. The child's small, round head had been shaved, and except for the dirty jacket which bound him to the slats, he was completely naked.

They heard sharp, quick footsteps coming. Joey motioned in desperation toward the mattress. They darted behind it just as Nurse Bonzer and the new boy came into the room.

Neither Tootie nor Joey dared move. They could hear the pathetic cries of the new admission as he was wrapped in a wet jacket and tied to a second bed in the room.

"When this jacket dries," Nurse Bonzer said as she cinched it tight, "it will get real snug. This will teach you not to bite!"

In the midst of all the commotion, Tootie and Joey heard some soft mumbling. "God . . . God . . . God," Number 63 repeated. The voice was weak and wheezy, but it was unmistakably Buddy's.

Tootie and Joey stared at each other. They were both ready to push away the mattress and storm into the room when Buddy repeated, "God . . . God . . . God."

"Shut up!" Nurse Bonzer screamed in fury. "Why are you talking about God when you're tied to those boards?" Then, to Tootie's and Joey's surprise, Nurse Bonzer's voice changed and she began to laugh. It was a hideous sound and it sent chills up and down Tootie's spine.

Finally Nurse Bonzer's laughter subsided. Then she said in a fiendish whisper, "Your God can't hear you, Number 63. He doesn't even know you're alive!"

"God . . . God . . . God," Buddy whispered.

Nurse Bonzer marched to and fro between the two beds, like a mad woman. The new inmate kept crying while strapped tightly in his wet-pack, and the other kept praying. Tootie and Joey clung to each other.

"Go ahead, you stupid boys," Nurse Bonzer hissed. "Make your noises—cry, scream, curse, pray. Yes, pray! No one's going to hear either one of you. No one cares—especially your God, Number 63!" Then Nurse Bonzer strode over to the door. "I'm not afraid of your worthless praying—even if Dr. Dunn is." Her wicked laugh echoed loudly as she shut and locked the door.

Without waiting, Tootie and Joey scrambled from behind the mattress. Tootie rushed over to Buddy, while Joey checked the door.

"Oh, Buddy Boy, what have they done to you?" Tootie cried.

Buddy's face was puffy and bruised. He kept whispering, "God."

With trembling hands, Tootie unknotted the straps of the jacket which held Buddy to the wooden slats. Very carefully she helped him sit, and then got him out of the horrible restraint. Lovingly she wrapped his body in her blanket.

"We're here, Buddy Boy," she whispered soothingly. "We've come to take you home." Then Tootie began to sob, "I'm so sorry we left you here. Oh, Buddy Boy, forgive us!"

Finally Buddy opened his swollen eyes and peeked through the puffy slits. He barely whispered, "Toot?"

"Yes, Buddy Boy, it's me! God heard your prayers! He sent me to rescue you!"

"And m-me, too," Joey added. He hurried over to the other bed and began untying the wet-pack. But Number 64 didn't understand. He must have thought something more was going to be done to him because he began screaming. Joey tried to hush the frightened child, but he was in a state of complete panic.

Neither Tootie nor Joey heard the key turning in the lock. The next thing they knew, Dr. Dunn, Nurse Bonzer, and Herman were standing in the open doorway. Tootie saw them first, and screamed, "Joey, watch out!"

As Joey turned, Herman knocked him clear across the room. Joey slammed into the mattress, broadside, and it fell down on top of him. Herman clawed his way over the top, while Joey crawled from underneath.

The moment Joey scrambled to his feet, Dr. Dunn grabbed him. "Quit all this fumbling!" the doctor demanded. He was glaring at Herman.

Herman swore.

Meanwhile, Nurse Bonzer had pulled Tootie away from her brother. "What should we do with them?" she demanded of Dr. Dunn. "We can't let them go!"

"You'd b-better!" Joey stammered.

Herman hit him on the side of his head.

Dr. Dunn stood in the middle of the room, thinking. "We have to clear out of here . . . tonight," he announced. "The authorities will be looking for these young people. I knew that McCarthy girl meant trouble from the moment I saw her." He glared at Tootie.

Nurse Bonzer violently yanked her arms behind her.

Dr. Dunn continued, "We'll tie them up, lock the place, take the money, and be long gone before anybody arrives. We've done it before."

"They'll be able to identify us!" Nurse Bonzer bellowed. "In the past it's always been our word against some lunatic's. We've got to shut these two up!"

"How?" Dr. Dunn asked as he nervously ran his moist hands through his peach-fuzz hair.

"How!" exclaimed Nurse Bonzer. "The only answer is to use the electric shock machine. You've read the reports as well as I have. It's believed that the electric current going through the brain makes the patient forget. If we do it to these two troublemakers, they'll forget everything they've seen."

"It's not safe," Dr. Dunn protested. Nevertheless, Tootie saw him almost grin at the suggestion. "Electroshock is still in the experimental stage," he continued.

"Then let's experiment!" Herman shouted, still holding Joey tightly.

Tootie tried pulling away from Nurse Bonzer, but it was impossible.

Buddy was too weak to help her or Joey. He lay back down on the slats and kept mumbling, "God . . . God . . . God."

"Make him stop!" Dr. Dunn demanded. "I want no more praying!"

Nurse Bonzer scoffed, and viciously twisted Tootie's arm. "Don't worry—they're just empty mumblings. There's no God to help him."

"There is, too!" Tootie shouted.

"Th-that's right!" Joey added.

"God . . . God . . . God," Buddy repeated.

"Shut them *all* up!" Dr. Dunn demanded.

Nurse Bonzer grinned as if she'd been given the wealth of the world on a silver platter. "That's *exactly* what I plan to do!" She began dragging Tootie out of the room.

Herman pulled Joey after them.

Once again, Buddy tried to get up, but he was too weak to stand. He fell back down on the slats and continued calling out to God.

"We'll do that one first," Nurse Bonzer said to Herman who was struggling with Joey.

"Hurry!" Dr. Dunn said impatiently. "We've got to get out of here."

Tootie felt as though she were in a terrible nightmare and couldn't wake up. She watched as Herman strapped Joey to the table in the middle of the corridor.

Joey kept kicking, thrashing his arms, and struggling with all his might. But, when he was completely strapped in place and the electric wires were attached to his head, he turned and stared at Tootie. Mingled with the fear, he had an unexpected look of trust. "I-I-I'll be all right," he said. Then he looked up at the ceiling as if he thought God were going to send some angel to rescue him.

Tootie desperately wanted to do something. Anything! But all she could think of was Pastor Myers's comment about being harmless as doves and as sneaky as snakes. She looked under the table and saw that one of the electric cords from the box with dials was dangling. It looked just like a snake. Tootie shouted, "Look! It's a snake!"

Nurse Bonzer momentarily loosened her hold. Tootie gave her a violent shove, darted to the table, and knocked the electroshock box onto the floor. She began stomping and trampling it until Herman grabbed her.

"Look what you've done!" he shouted. "The machine's ruined!" He backhanded Tootie across the face. Nurse Bonzer strode toward her.

Just then the door at the end of the corridor burst open. Police officers stormed into the room, followed close behind by Tootie's and Joey's parents. And directly behind them were Pearl and Pastor Myers.

The following minutes were filled with confusion for Tootie. She watched as Dr. Dunn, Nurse Bonzer, and Herman were arrested. She saw the leather straps and electric wires being removed from Joey. She heard him tell everyone how God had led them right into Fairbolt, and how God and Tootie had rescued him from the electroshock machine. Tootie watched the inmates being released from their rooms and carefully guided out of the asylum.

Pearl and Mother were hugging Buddy and trying to comfort him. Pastor Myers was praising God that the McCarthys had discovered Tootie's absence and had notified the Staddlers, the police, and himself in time to save everyone. Tootie even noticed her father frantically searching through the lobby desk and then stuffing a check into his pocket. He nodded at her with satisfaction, as if it had been she who had saved the Specialty Pie Bakery and the future of their family.

It wasn't, however, until everyone was standing outside by the Model T that Tootie started coming out of her stupor. Pearl repeatedly asked, "What are you going to do with the reward, Tootie?"

"Reward?"

"Yes, silly, you're the heroine," Pearl giggled.

"Me?"

"Yes, lass," Mother added. "You've not only saved our Buddy from more harm than was already done to him, but many other children as well. We're proud of you, Tootie."

Father was lovingly holding Buddy in his arms. Buddy was wrapped snuggly in several blankets. "Our lad's hair will grow back and his bruises will fade," Father said, looking down at his son. "And from now on he'll be safe at home with us."

Buddy began rubbing the material of the blanket between his fingers.

Just then Officer Riley passed and mentioned that they would need to come down to the station tomorrow for more details. Then he proceeded to lead the handcuffed Dr. Dunn, Nurse Bonzer, Herman, and Charles away.

Buddy whispered, "God . . . God . . . God!"

Dr. Dunn shouted, "Shut that boy up! For pity's sake . . . make that stupid Number 63 stop praying!"

Nurse Bonzer spit at them.

Herman glared.

Charles was crying.

Tootie looked away, her thin lips quivering. "I'm so glad we never have to see them again!"

Pastor Myers interjected gently, "They need the Lord, Tootie. They were certainly wolves in sheep's clothing. But maybe no one has ever told them of God's love."

"I never thought about that," she admitted. "But I do know that God loves our Buddy Boy." She reached out and touched his cheek. "God heard our Buddy's prayers, and he sent us to rescue him."

"Th-that's right!" Joey added.

The tension began to ease.

Pastor Myers stepped close. "Remember what I told you about how God turns bad situations around. Well, those scoundrels meant all of this for evil. But God, in his infinite wisdom, is turning it around for good."

Tootie and Joey nodded thoughtfully.

They continued watching as the culprits were put into a patrol car. With lights flashing and siren blaring, they were driven past the crab apple tree out the Fairbolt gate.

Then the McCarthys, Staddlers, and Pastor Myers watched as all the frightened Fairbolt inmates were loaded into vehicles by more policemen. They were going to a safe place, the authorities had promised.

Finally Eve said in a whisper, "God is good!"

"He certainly is!" their pastor said.

"That's right!" Tootie agreed. "And I think me and Joey learned to trust God tonight."

Joey grinned and then added, "Even if we were s-scared to death!"

Everyone laughed.

Tootie continued, "I want to use the reward money to get a real doctor for Buddy and for Mother. And then I want to pay someone to help us in the house, just like Pastor Myers suggested—so Mama can get some rest."

Eve smiled gently.

Father moved a step closer to Tootie. He was still holding Buddy in his arms, and they looked down into his sleeping face. Then they looked at each other and smiled. "You'll be receiving one thousand dollars, lass. That's a handsome reward."

"What else are you going to do with it?" Pearl asked. Her front teeth moved up and down as she looked wistfully at her younger sister.

Tootie smiled and then said, "Would you like to go to a dentist?"

Pearl squealed excitedly. "Would I!" she cried and then she hugged Tootie, Father, Buddy, Mother, Pastor Myers, and even Joey.

God really is making everything turn out good, Tootie thought and sighed contentedly.